TORTURED crown

A FORBIDDEN AGE GAP ROMANCE

ELEANOR ALDRICK

TORTURED
crown

A FORBIDDEN AGE GAP ROMANCE

ELEANOR ALDRICK

Tortured Crown
Copyright © 2022 by Eleanor Aldrick
All rights reserved.

Cover Design: Sinfully Seductive Designs
Interior Formatting: Sinfully Seductive Designs
Proof Read by: OnPointeDigitalServices

No part of this book may be reproduced in any form or by any electronic or mechanical means, including information storage and retrieval systems, without written permission from the author, except for the use of brief quotations in a book review.

For more information, address: eleanoraldrick@gmail.com

This is a work of fiction. Names, characters, businesses, places, events, locales, and incidents are either the products of the author's imagination or used in a fictitious manner. Any resemblance to actual persons, living or dead, or actual events is purely coincidental.

ISBN No. 979-8-3302-8785-7
FIRST EDITION
10 9 8 7 6 5 4 3 2 1

For all those who seek escape.
I've got you.

Over-the-top, possessive men.
They may not be ideal in the real world, *but damn*, are they hot on paper.
-Eleanor Aldrick

ON REPEAT
playlist

Harmless - Grey Ziegler
Never Enough - **Bryce Savage**
Escort - Nikitata
Going, Going, Gone - **Luke Combs**
Gato de Noche - Nengo Flow & Bad Bunny
Make it Hot - **Major Later & Anitta**
You Know the Drill - Andy Mineo
Jaded - **Drake**
Good People - Rhys Lewis
Beautiful Day - **Trinix, Rushawn & Jermaine Edwards**
Half Grown - Zach Bryan
Heartache Medication - **Jon Pardi**

PLAYLIST

Condemned - Zach Bryan
Fall in Love with You - **Montell Fish**
Heartless - Diplo Feat. Morgan Wallen
Forever - **Jesse Reyes**
Look at Her Now - Selena Gomez
We Ride - **Bryan Martin**

Prologue
HAYLEY

FIVE YEARS AGO...

"What do you mean *she isn't mine*?"

Those last three words loop in my head, drowning out the corresponding sobs.

"Parker, I swear it's not what you think." She pleads while kneeling at his feet, her hands outstretched and reaching.

"I don't care what you say. This is unforgivable." There's a loud pounding, and I'm unsure if it's Father's doing or my own damn pulse. "The amount of money I've spent on that girl. She was poised to take over my empire, Miranda. You think I'm going to let your indiscretion oversee my dynasty?"

And if his words weren't enough to shatter my heart, my mother's surely do.

"Wait! Please wait!" She shuffles toward his retreating frame, her next words taking my heart right along with them. "She isn't mine either."

Silence. Dead silence fills the room.

"What?" It's barely audible, but I can feel Father's derision from my crouched position in the hall.

"Please, Parker. Understand… We'd been trying for so long. Nothing kept happening." Mother sniffles as her eyes fall in shame. "I was leaving the doctor's office when I was approached by this man. He said that he'd gladly help me out with our *problem*."

"Problem? What the hell are you talking about, woman!?" Father spits out, his eyes laser focused on the crumpled form beneath him. "You were pregnant. I saw you with my own eyes!"

At this, Mother cackles. "Did you? Did you, really? You disappeared as soon as I started 'showing.' Said it weirded you out to touch me when I was in that *state*." For the first time since this confrontation started, Mother is the one who looks repulsed. "It was easy to hide it from you, let you think that my pregnancy was going as planned, when you weren't even around to fully witness it."

Father's eyes narrow as he crouches before her. "So, what? What are you saying?"

"I bought her. She's ours. Not some indiscretion you should discard." Father scoffs at her words, only serving to anger her. "Parker, she's still our daughter!"

"My daughter, my ass. Did you stop to think of the repercussions should her biological parents come after her? She doesn't have our blood, Miranda. How stupid can you be? How could you risk our reputation like that, buying a baby off the black market? Do you have any idea what this will do to us if it gets out?!"

My chest tightens as tears prickle my eyes, the reality of their words finally sinking in. *I'm not theirs. They aren't mine.*

"The man assured me it would never get out." Mother wrings her hands, her gaze falling on the ground once more.

"Stupid woman. The truth always comes out."

"She's our daughter, Parker. She's worth the risk!"

Father sneers as he rises to his full height, "She's a fucking liability, Miranda! Definitely not worth the *risk.*" With that last word, he shakes mother off his leg, the leg she'd been clinging onto for dear life. As if he were her savior, the one to abolish her of her sins.

Me. I'm the sin. The risk. The liability.

A choked sob escapes me, and my silent perch in the hall is no longer a secret.

"*Hayley?*" Mother's tortured voice breaks me from my

trance, our eyes clashing with a mixture of pain and sorrow. We both know. Nothing she can say or do will erase what I've just learned, but that doesn't stop her from trying. "I'm so sorry, baby."

Her voice is growing distant despite her stepping closer. *I can't breathe.* The walls are closing in on me, and my chest is threatening to implode.

With a mind of their own, my feet turn me away from their view. *I can't bear it.* The mixture of shame and disgust riddling their faces is just too much.

"*Hayley! Wait!*" Mother's shouts trail off as the cold night air meets my face.

I don't know where I'm going or what I'm going to do. All I know is that I need to get away from this pain, this ache that's eating me alive.

My knees buckle as the air gets thicker and my vision starts to haze. *What the fuck is this? A heart attack?*

Maybe. Maybe I've died from a broken heart, the bright lights paving my way to heaven. Yes. That's it. That must be it.

I close my eyes, ready to surrender.

"Hayley! Get out of the—"

Hands dig into my ribs before I'm being flung to the side. The sound of screeching tires and a blood-curdling scream is the last thing I hear before I'm ripped back into reality.

Oh god, no! What have I done?

"*Miranda!*" Father races to the lifeless body before me,

where blood pools around it like a dark hole ready to take it under. "Look what you've done, you useless—"

"I—I'm sorry, so sorry." My words are barely audible, the pounding in my ear mixing with the shrieking off to the right.

And like the flip of a switch, a blanket of cold settles over me. The pain, it's gone. All that's left is this empty hollow, growing with every drop of inky blood I see. Blood. Blood that's not mine. Blood spilled that I could never repay.

"*Oh, Jesus.* Stay with me, woman. You aren't leaving me with your abomination." Even as the light leaves her eyes, he shames her, his body hovering over hers like some sort of grim reaper.

"This is *your* mess, Miranda." He brings a cell phone to his ear, something I'd completely missed before. "Yes, I'm still on the line, but you better hurry. I'm not sure how much time she has left. She's losing a lot of blood." A beat passes before his eyes lift to mine. "No, I'm not a match... and neither is our *daughter*."

The disdain in his voice isn't lost on me, and deservedly so.

I did this. This is all my fault, and there's no way my useless blood could save her now.

Crawling back to Mother, I lay at her feet, not daring to move her an inch. And with every fiber of my being, I pray —pray that whatever powers that be take me instead of her, the woman that raised me as her own.

I don't have any of the answers to the questions rattling off in my head. All I have are the memories this woman gave me. All with her unconditional love and support. *She can't die. She just can't.*

Minutes that feel like hours pass before help finally arrives, but it's too late. I fear Mother is gone, and Father is already planning on covering up the truth. My mind is numb as I sit here, covered in her blood, unable to process the reality of the situation.

As the paramedics load into the ambulance, my father turns to me, his face devoid of emotion. It's clear that any trace of the love he once had for me is gone.

"*Let's go,*" he growls, but I don't move—*can't move*—as he grabs me by the arm, pulling me away from the only mother I've ever known. I stumble along beside him, feeling nothing but a sense of emptiness as he leads me to his car.

And as we drive behind the blaring truck, I can't help but wonder what my future holds. Will I be cast aside like some dirty secret, or will my father continue to use me for his own gain? *I don't know.*

But as I sit in the car surrounded by the stench of death and my own guilt, I can't shake the feeling that my life is forever changed.

I'm no longer their daughter. I'm no longer a Barclay.

Chapter One
MATTHEW

"Stop being a prude, brother." Radley rolls his eyes as he makes himself a drink behind my personal bar.

"Do that shit one more time and I'm kicking your ass right out of this building. Don't try me. And don't call me *brother*."

I have four of them already. I don't need this knuckle head added to the mix.

"Come on, bro—I mean Matt. I'm just trying to break you out of this funk you're in. Don't think the team hasn't noticed."

I sigh as I run a hand through my hair, tugging at the

ends. "I get it that things have been tense lately, but they always are this time of year."

Yes, it's true that the end of the year is hectic for those of us in the liquor industry, and it doesn't help that I have this pompous prick trying to buy up most of the company's shares, pestering me every opportunity he gets—but if I were being honest with myself, my issues run deeper than just work.

I'm restless. All but one of my brothers have found their match. *Their soulmates.* I scoff. They're delusional.

Still. Something's missing and I can't help but think that they're onto something.

"One little outing isn't going to kill you. Besides, it's to one of your own establishments. Think of it as an extension of work." He lifts his glass toward me in cheers, but his face sours almost instantly. "Oh, I get it...the boss man is too big to go out with his peons."

I cackle at this, my head tilting back in a throaty laugh. "You are anything but a damn peon. You make enough money to start your own whiskey distillery, Radley."

"Fat chance I'd be the success you are." He hands me a rocks glass of my private label, Tortured Crown, the oak notes hitting me as soon as I take it.

"Well, Razz, on that we can agree." I smirk before taking a sip of the amber liquid, the smooth warmth trickling down my throat a nice welcome.

"Come on. Just one outing and I promise I'll drop it."

I raise a brow, knowing this man to never give up one

inch. It's what makes him one of my best in sales and one of the reasons I'm in every major venue this side of the hemisphere. I've only had him on board for a couple of months and already he's made such a difference.

Yes, he's a fucking sleaze bag. But that's part of what makes him so good at his job.

Would I trust him with smoothly talking his way into a new contract? Yes. Would I trust him around any female I cared about? *Fuck no*. He may be older, but I've never seen anyone pull ass like him. So yeah, that'd be a *hard no*.

"Fine." I press the cold glass to my forehead. "But after tonight, you drop it."

"Hell yeah! You won't regret it, boss. I've got the perfect girl I've been dying to set you up with."

"Oh, no. No way in hell I'm letting you set me up with one of your disease infested hookups." I put the tumbler down on the table a little harder than intended, the contents spilling onto the wood desk and tingeing it a darker shade of brown. "Look, no offense, but your taste in women isn't exactly discriminatory and I still haven't forgotten that one time you caught the clap."

He turns a deep red, something I've never seen before. "Hey, everybody makes mistakes, right? Anyway, this girl won't give me the time of day. She's a good girl, I swear?"

I snort, "Oh, yeah? And how'd you meet her? I know it wasn't at Sunday service."

"The details of how don't really matter." His eyes quickly track from left to right as he mumbles something under his breath. "All you need to know is that she's as pure as the snow is white."

I choke on my spit. "Fuck no. I'm steering clear of that hot mess. Virgins are a no go for me. They get attached and are all clingy. Definitely not what I'm looking for right now."

He shrugs and a beat passes before what he said sinks in further. I know he's a sleaze, but... "Do I even want to know how you became privy to such delicate information in the first place?"

"Nah, you don't, so I'll spare you the details." He runs a hand through his long hair, his eyes focusing intently on the wall to his right. "Look, I'm not asking you to marry this girl. Just meet her. If she doesn't float your boat, then no harm, no foul."

I roll my eyes. The way he's talking up this girl, you'd think he actually cared. "Fine. But if we're doing this, we're doing it now. The sooner we get this night over with, the better."

Radley waggles his brows. "You won't be saying that after you meet her. You'll be wanting this outing to last *all* night long."

I sigh into my glass before downing the remnants of my drink, letting the sting of the alcohol set the tone for the hot mess that's sure to come.

That's her. It has to be.

She sticks out like a nun in a whorehouse. But, God. *Those lips*. Those lips were made for nothing but sin.

Like a bat to the head, explicit images hit me—her delicate knees hitting the ground as those plump pillows of pink stretch around my thick girth, sliding in ever so slowly...

A shove to my shoulder shakes me from my fantasy and I can't help but growl.

"Ha, I see you've spotted the little dove." Radley's slimy gaze falls on her and I want nothing more than to gouge his eyes out.

"How?" I grab at his collar, the action making him face me and temporarily abating my inner rage.

"How what?" Radley's brows furrow, clearly as confused as I am.

I don't act out. Rarely become physical unless provoked. But the mere thought of him having had a taste of that pretty little thing is sending me on a downward spiral.

"How did you meet her? And so help me God, if you say you've laid one of those grimy fingers on her..."

"No, boss. No! I swear." His brows squeeze together further, his eyes searching mine—perhaps for the sanity that's clearly left my body and is nowhere to be found. On a rushed breath, Radley feebly attempts to reassure me once more, "She doesn't like me, wouldn't give me the time of day. Figured me out from the get, called me a *fuckboy* if I recall."

I snort. The thought of someone putting Radley in his place makes me laugh. But such filthy words coming out of such a pretty mouth just doesn't compute.

Needing to investigate further, I finally loosen my grip on Radley, and his audible sigh of relief isn't lost on me. *Wow.* What in the world's come over me?

But with every step I take toward this vision in white, I know exactly what it is. It's her, everything about her. From the way she writes in her notebook to the way her long legs are crossed beneath that fitted cream dress, it all screams sex in the most innocent way. *Like a ripe peach, ready for the picking.*

As if sensing me, her eyes lift from the journal she'd been writing in. *Breathtaking.* Her chocolate brown collide with mine and I'm lost, lost in the paralyzing sensation. It's not until she licks her lips and my gaze drops down to that pout, that I've realized I've stopped short of pressing myself against her lithe frame.

"Ah, um. Do I know you?" Her voice shakes and the sudden urge to wrap my arms around her becomes as instinctive as my need for air. It takes everything in me to take a step back, giving her a modicum of space, but it isn't easy.

God, I hope I haven't scared her. Clearing my throat, I try to relax into the bar, dropping down my six-foot-three frame just a tad and exhaling a gravelly, "No."

"*Oh.*" She blinks up at me, her cheeks tingeing the prettiest shade of pink, and it takes every ounce of self-restraint I have not to bite them right here and now.

Extending a hand, I attempt to assemble a sentence. "You'll have to excuse me. I'm not usually such a Neanderthal. But it's not every day I come across such beauty."

Her cheeks turn a deeper shade as she takes my hand in hers and the jolt is immediate. It's obvious she feels this too.

Instinctively, I pull her hand closer until the back of her hand is hovering just below my lips. Everything inside of me is screaming at me to stop, to step away from this innocent dove and let her fly. *But fuck if I can.* Doing something selfish for once in my life, I let my lips brush the softest skin I've ever had the privilege of feeling.

My God, she feels this too.

Our eyes clash and I catch the shiver she tries to hide. *I affect her.* Maybe not as much as she does me, but I do.

I let my vision trail down to her delicate neck, the skin begging to be licked, and down further past the high collar of her dress. Unfortunately for her, her perky breasts give her away. They're pressed up against the fabric of her dress and the tightening of her perfect nipples are like two beacons calling me home. I need them in my mouth. *Right-the-fuck-now.*

I blink. Once. Twice. *Jesus. Get a hold of yourself.* Shaking myself out of this lust induced haze, I finally release her hand from my hold and allow it to drop gently onto her lap.

It's the dry spell I've had. *Nothing more*. But even as I feed myself this twisted logic, I know it isn't true. I've gone longer without sex and haven't been driven to such insanity.

She's a siren. She must be. The quicker I get her out of my system the quicker I can get back to my normal routine.

Doing something completely out of turn, I act on impulse and grip onto either side of her tiny waist. Before I can think better of it, I'm plucking her from her seat and pressing her to me.

God, she smells like heaven, and I know I need more. "Baby, I need to taste you, drink your honey, feel your thighs shake around my face."

She gasps, her small frame pushing harder into mine out of her own volition and I swear that alone threatens to make my knees buckle.

Her fingers dig into me just then and the bite on my taught biceps serve as a welcome reminder of our current setting. I can't let myself get too carried away, because given time, I'd rut into her like a wild animal—onlookers be damned.

"So what's it gonna be, doll? You letting me taste you?"

She tilts her head back, and with eyes full of heat and desire, she gives me the greatest gift. "Okay."

That's it. Just one word and I swear it feels as if she's served me the seven wonders.

"Okay," I repeat on a whisper.

I'm not sure what I've done in this life to deserve this opportunity, but I'm sure as hell not going to waste it spending another second in this bar.

Making haste, I drop one of my hands from around her waist while pressing the other to the small of her back, ushering her toward the exit.

"But wait. My tab, my friend, my bag—" She looks toward her seat where a gray leather satchel sits.

With my free hand, I scoop it up before signaling to the bartender. One quick nod letting him know she's under my care.

Whatever this girl wants for or needs, she'll have while visiting any Tortured Crown establishment. This one being no exception.

My doll looks between the bartender and me, her brows furrowing quizzically, but she fails to ask a question. No matter. There'll be time for that later. Right now? Right now, *I'm taking her home.*

Chapter Two
HAYLEY

It's okay, Hayley. You deserve this. You deserve this bit of joy.

I kept up that constant pep talk all the way here. I've never in my life done anything like this. Heck, I've never so much as kissed a boy, let alone a man. And that's exactly what my handsome stranger is. *All man.*

Broad and tall, chiseled and demanding. There's no way I could turn him down. Not when a single touch of his skin silenced all the chaos inside me.

He's magic. At least I want to think he is. And for one night, that's what I'll let myself have.

Yes, I was supposed to be working for my father, but screw it. I'm allowed one reckless night. One brief glimpse of joy.

And that's exactly what I feel with him. The way this man looks at me, the way he touches me. It inspires nothing but warmth and joy.

No matter what we've been doing, he's had to maintain constant contact with my body, making me feel cherished. Whether it was his hand on my thigh in the car, his hand on the small of my back upon entering his home, or like now—he's twirling me around before pulling my chest to his, his head tilting toward the corner of the room where there's a bar setup.

"Care for a drink, doll?"

My heart is beating a mile a minute as I soak in his features under the soft yellow light. He's so much older than me, something father would never approve of. And if I were being honest with myself, the knowledge of that thrills me to no end. Despite that, I can't hide the truth about my age, so I answer the best way I can. "No, thank you. Not unless you want to facilitate underage drinking."

His body tenses before me, and a frown mars his full lips. "I'm sorry, what? What did you say?"

He's clearly concerned but has yet to let go of my waist, so I go for broke and tell him the truth. Worst thing he can do is kick me out, right?

"I'm twenty."

His lips part and eyes narrow. "But your hips…" He

grips them tight, "And these tits…" He stares at them as if they hold the answers to life's greatest secrets. "Your body. It's all woman. And you were at the bar…"

"Yeah, about that—"

"*Christ*. Radley's gonna pay for this shit," he mutters before bringing me flush against his body, pressing his lips to the top of my head. "Look, doll. If you were any other girl… I've got two hard and fast rules. I don't do virgins and I don't do teenagers."

He finally releases me, and I feel like weeping from the loss. Needing to feel his touch once more, I do something so out of character and go after what I want.

I close the distance between us, running the palms of my hands up his firm chest and revel in the hiss he gives me.

My stranger raises a brow before grabbing a hold of my hips. "Baby, you're playing with fire."

"Maybe I want to get burned." I slowly walk forward until the back of his knees hit the leather sofa. "And I'm *not* a teenager. I'm all woman."

I place both palms on his chest and gently push, watching him fall back. Seeing the opportunity for what it is, I straddle him where he sits.

"Little girl, twenty is just shy from nine*teen*." His chest is heaving now, and the knowledge that I'm the one making him react this way gives me a confidence I've never had before. "Stop. I already gave you a warning."

"And maybe I don't care about your warning." I lower

myself until our bodies are pressed together, and *oh god... is that... is that his dick?*

A soft mewl escapes me as I rock back and forth, the pressure building with every pivot and making my eyes roll back in my head.

I'm lost in a haze when a dark chuckle lets me know I have an audience. And when I return my gaze to his, I see nothing but possession lingering in his eyes.

"Is this your first time riding cock, little doll?"

I can't lie. Not to him.

Nibbling on my bottom lip, I nod, this knowledge only making him groan a deep, painful sound.

"Jesus." He grips my face with both of his masculine hands and brings our lips a hair's breadth apart. "You'll be the death of me. Sending me straight to Hell."

His words send a shiver down my back, like some sort of sensual omen. But we must all come to an end, and if this is one way of going into the dark abyss, then I'm all for it.

"Good. Take me with you." I whisper into his parted lips before licking along the seam.

"Siren. You're a fucking siren." Primal noises emanate from his mouth, now tightly sealed over mine. And with unleashed restraint, he grips my head, fingers digging into my scalp before devouring my mouth whole.

Oh, God. This feels so good. His velvety soft tongue dancing with mine, the heat building inside of me. And this pressure in my core? I need to move. *I can't stay still.*

The tickle intensifies as I roll my hips, and when the top of his ridge bumps against my swollen clit, I can't hold back the moan.

Never in my life have I felt this way. Even when I've touched myself, it all paled in comparison.

"That's it, baby. Keep rocking, just like that." His fingers trail down my neck, over my shoulders and down to my collarbone before he's cupping my breasts in a firm embrace. "Tell you what. You rub that sweet little cunt all over my hard length, and we'll get you to cum. But that's it. I can't let it go any further."

"Are you trying to bargain with me?" I gyrate on this man's lap, my thoughts all in shambles. I'm pretty sure he could get me to hop on one leg right now, and I'd happily do it. *Anything to keep this sensation going.* Either way, I'm not going to make it easy on him. I run my fingers up his hard chest, up the column of his throat, and into his full head of hair. "Because, you know, I could do this…" I lick a line up his throat and feel his cock pulse against my slit. "All night. Torture you until you have no choice but to cum right along with me."

"Fuck, baby. I'm trying to be a good man." He digs his fingers into my hips as he thrusts up, my head falling back from the friction as I moan out in pleasure. "But you're making it *really* hard."

"Perfect. That's just how I want it." I let one of my hands trail down to his large bulge before giving it a little squeeze. "Nice and *hard.*"

My stranger moans as his hands find my ass, his fingers digging into the meaty flesh. "Baby doll, I warned you, and now you're gonna pay."

"*Good.*" I sigh, ready to pay whatever price for a ride on my Greek god. "When do we star—"

My words falter as he rips off my thong, the fabric roughly grazing my sex and making me whimper. "You're gonna cum for me, doll, get that cream all over my fingers. I need to taste you."

Oh, God. I mewl as he takes his digits and swipes them along my slick heat, his eyes going positively molten.

"I may not be able to fuck you, but I sure as hell am going to enjoy you." The pads of his fingers rub slow circles around my clit and my entire body trembles. I'm a live wire. So close to release. "Christ, your little cunt is soaked. It'd be so easy for me to slide inside that tight little hole."

Just then he teases me, gently inserting the top of his fat digit into my core.

"*Oh, lord. Oh, God.*" I'm clenching around him, my walls choking his finger, wanting to suck him in. *I want more. I need more.*

"Tell me, baby. Has this been claimed?" Possession dances in his eyes as the tip of his finger continues to thrust in and out. "Are you untouched?"

My bottom lip trembles and I know I can't lie to him, so I whisper, "Yes."

His eyes squeeze shut, and his head falls back with a roar. "*Fuuuuuck.*"

Fear clogs my throat, and I wonder if he's about to send me home. I know this is crazy, but everything in me is begging for me to stay.

He removes his hand from my core and brings it to his mouth before sucking the fingers clean.

"Of course you'd taste amazing," he groans. "Look, doll. There's no going back. There's no way I'd let another man have you. Not after having you on me, feeling your heat and tasting your honey."

"*You want me?*" My chest swells and I feel pressure build behind my lids.

"Of course I want you. Every hot-blooded man would want you. But none of them would deserve you." The back of his hand reverently brushes my cheek. "Hell, *I* don't even deserve you. But that's not stopping me from taking this precious gift."

Gift. He thinks I'm a gift.

I'm swooning hard. Yes, men have said similar things to me in the past, but none of them have evoked feelings like this.

A phone rings off in the distance and the man beneath me groans. "*Damnit.*"

"Everything okay?" My brows furrow as I feel his body tense.

"Yeah. It's the office line. They wouldn't be calling unless it were an emergency." He sighs as he places his hands on my waist, lifting me off of him before lowering me onto the couch. "I'll be right back, doll."

He places a kiss on my forehead before disappearing into the hall, and I swear I melt right into the leather.

But one minute quickly turns into two, and with every tick of the clock, I have more room to think. Now that he's not beneath me, everything is losing its lust-filled haze.

I'm in shock. *What in the heck am I doing?!* I have no business seducing an older man. *None.* And I left Melissa behind at the bar. I'm sure she thinks I'm a shitty friend.

She knew I was dreading the trip to The Fox and offered to tag along for moral support. Said she'd been there tons of times and was even friends with the bartender.

God, I hope she understands.

I'm never taken aback by men. They aren't even on my radar. But as soon as my eyes clashed with the broody stranger, it was as if I were in a trance. Everything in me was begging to surrender, to let his powerful hands roam, letting his touch soothe the deep ache I hold inside.

"Ha!" I scoff. *As if any one person held that kind of power.*

A soft click signals a door shutting in the distance, and the sound threatens to make my heart pound right out of my chest. *This is it.* My chance to cut tail and run or stay and find out what the fuss is all about.

I've never had a boyfriend, much less laid with a man. Father forbade it. Said it would ruin any prospects of landing a good catch. *And there it is, the real reason for my change of heart.* No matter what I do, his voice creeps in and ruins it all.

I roll my eyes, wondering if I'll ever grow a backbone and stand up to that asshole for once.

Well, like they say—*if not now, then never.*

I take in a deep breath before letting it out slowly. This is it. This is when I take my life back. I'm doing what I want, and it all starts with that handsome stranger.

It's perfect. He doesn't know who I am or who my father is. It'll be a simple transaction. *Purely pleasure.*

Heck, he even said he didn't do virgins. The way I see it, I'll be doing him a favor.

Needing a distraction, I let my wobbly legs take me toward the bookshelf nestled in the lounge's corner. The room is opulent, with its leather tufted sectional and the intricate wood paneling. It doesn't take a genius to see he's done well for himself. Or at the very least, comes from money.

Blech. The first flaw I see.

Don't get me wrong, I have nothing against money, per se. It's just that it's typically tied to ruthless men—*men like my father.*

Right on cue, bile churns in my stomach, overtaking the butterflies that had resided there just moments ago.

"*Enough!*" I whisper-hiss into the silent room, letting my gaze land on a picture frame sitting on the bar. "Wow. They're all beautiful."

My eyes scan all five men and two women. They're

absolutely stunning, all dressed in formal-wear and surrounding a happy couple—clearly a bride and groom.

Yes, they're all GQ and Vogue material, but what's most striking is the look on their faces. *Happiness.* Something I'm not sure I've ever truly experienced.

I let my thumb caress the image of joy personified, letting myself imagine what it would be like if I were there with them. Would I too have that same look on my face? Would my heart finally feel complete?

My eyes prickle and a deep pitted feeling settles in my stomach as an old memory bubbles up.

"Stop that, Hayley. You know life has something else in store. You owe a debt, and people like you don't have the freedom to feel such trivial things like joy."

"It's just a party, Dad. There won't even be any guys involved." *I wring my hands, eyes focused intently on the ground.* *"Mila and Mel said so. Promised it was just a girl's night in, watching rom-coms and doing mani-pedis."*

Father scoffs. *"You don't need those girls to do your nails, child. I pay to keep you groomed. You do your nails and hair every two weeks—hiding that mousy brown that runs nowhere in our family."* *He pours himself some more whiskey before pointing the glass in my direction.* *"You know, that should've been the first tell-tale that you weren't really mine."*

I should be used to his rejection by now, but the sting

never lessens. It's true what he's saying. At least the part of me owing a debt, one I'm not sure I'll ever be able to repay, no matter how hard I try.

The creaking of a door snaps me out of my trip down memory lane and, with shaky hands, I place the picture frame back on its perch. It's then I see my stranger's wallet. His driver's license is clipped to the back, exposing his piercing hazel eyes.

I'm entranced. The sharp line of his masculine jaw paired with the warm tone of his skin are begging for a closer look. I know better but decide to skip my manners anyway. I pick up the wallet and bring the tiny square closer to my face.

God, he's breathtaking. I let my eyes shift to the right since it's only fair I know the name of the man I'm about to bed. Should probably text Melissa and let her know who I'm with too.

Yes, she's probably worried—*Wait. What? This can't be…*

Oh my fucking God. It is. It's Matthew Crown.

How could I be so stupid? Of course he'd be the mystery stranger.

With a shudder of disgust, I fling the wallet.

"This would make Father so happy. Me being in the lair of his latest hunted prize." I murmur to myself as I walk toward my bag, picking it up before I tiptoe out of this man's home.

There's no way in hell I'm giving my father this win, letting him hold it over Mr. Crown's head and demand some sort of repayment for taking his *daughter's* virtue.

Screw that. I may owe that man a debt, but it'll be a cold day in hell before I let him rope anyone else into being part of my sacrificial offering.

With a heavy heart, I close the door behind me and sigh. I've never in my life felt an attraction toward a man like I did Mr. Crown. So of course, it would make sense that Fate's sick and twisted humor would find a reason to deny me that bit of joy—the vile witch teasing me with a taste of what I'll never have.

Well, screw you, Fate. Screw you and screw my father.

Chapter Three
MATTHEW

"I don't want to hear it." I lift a hand up, palm exposed as I walk into my office, Radley's beady eyes and toothy grin following me in silence until I take a seat behind my large desk.

It's not until I've turned my monitor on that he musters the courage to speak. "But—"

"I *said* I don't want to hear it." I stare him down until he's nodding, acknowledging that I will have none of his bullshit this morning.

Very slowly I turn toward the massive window, refusing Radley the satisfaction of watching the discomfort on my face.

"All you need to know is that you are never to mention that girl again. She's as good as dead to me. Understood?"

"But boss—" he starts up again, but I'm not having it.

"Understood?!" I swing my head violently, landing a penetrating stare right through his soul. "As good as *dead*."

Radley audibly gulps, his head moving up and down like a damn bobble doll. "Understood."

"Good. Now get out. I've got shit to do."

With hurried steps, Radley maneuvers out of my office and it's not until after he's softly shut the door behind him that I let out a sigh of relief.

It stings. The knowledge that I was conned by my little doll. *"Ha,"* I scoff. She isn't my anything.

She's nothing more than a thief. A liar. And I was the fool that left my wallet out, ready for the taking.

Girl didn't even have the decency to leave the wallet and just take the money. No, she had to take everything, including the leather keepsake—a Christmas present from my niece, Penelope.

Fuck if I'll make that mistake again. No, soulmates and love at first sight are a myth. What a crock of shit. *My brothers have it all wrong.*

Speaking of the assholes, I need to check up on Hunter. He's been off on one of his solo trips and I'd be lying if I said I wasn't worried about him.

He's the only other Crown brother without a mate, and usually he's more cynical about love than me, but I saw the way he looked at Austin and Anaya when they were getting hitched.

I hadn't seen that type of longing in him since we were kids and Dad had denied him that '72 Corvette.

The line rings twice before Hunter picks up his SAT phone. "Yo."

"Yo? Is that any way to greet your twin brother?"

"I'm climbing turkey mountain right now, hanging on with one hand. What the fuck do you want, an extended monologue on the past forty-eight hours?"

"Jesus. Good to see your sarcasm is still intact. Hang up the phone and call me when you can. What I've got to say isn't worth plummeting to your death over."

There's some static and scuffling of fabric before Hunter grunts out his response. "There. I'm safe. Perched on a ledge. Now tell me what's up. You never call me unless something's up."

I blink, letting his words penetrate. He's right. We're not really big talkers, so why did I call? Surely, my questioning whether his love life was satisfactory could've waited until our next reunion.

"Matthew, talk. You're worrying me, brother."

"Shit, I guess I don't know. Sorry to bother."

"Ah, hell no. You can't hide from me. Do I need to cut this trip short, or are you going to come clean with it?"

Blowing out a long breath, I let him into the recesses of my mind. "Nothing, really. I was just worried about you. Saw the way you looked at Austin and Anaya, thought it seemed like you were envious of what they had, is all."

"Hmm."

"That's it? That's all you're going to say in response to that?"

"Yes. Seems to me like you're projecting, brother. Are *you* envious of what they have?"

I sputter. "Of being tied down for the rest of my life? Having to bend backwards to make a woman happy, a woman who'll likely steal my wallet and leave me all fucked up. *Nah.* No thanks."

Hunter snorts. "Your wallet? That's random. If anything, she'd make like Blanca and try to milk our family fortune dry."

It's not until he's repeating my own words that it hits me. There she is. The little doll sneaking back into my thoughts. Why else would I be bringing up my damn wallet?

Hunter keeps talking, despite my lack of response. "Look, as soon as I'm done with this climb, I'm coming home. It's obvious something's up with you."

I shake my head and take in a deep breath. "No, seriously. I was the one worried about you. Take your time. Sorry to bother."

"Ah, no you don't. You don't get to call me like this and then drop out when the conversation gets a little difficult. It's clear you're having some sort of emotional crisis. First you call me out of the blue, and then you're randomly talking about women stealing, as if they were all a carbon copy of our brother's evil ex."

"Aren't they though?" I spit out, instantly regretting it.

"No, they aren't. But you already know that." There's a pause before he's sighing into the phone. "Which is why I'm coming home. Whatever it is you're going through, brother, you're not doing it alone."

I swallow, but the lump in my throat refuses to go away. To be honest, this type of brotherly love is one I'm blessed to have. All of the Crown men are.

I may not have a fucking soulmate, but at least life has granted me four amazing brothers, and for that I am grateful.

Chapter Four
HAYLEY

"Thank you for picking me up and letting me crash here last night." I pull the mug of steaming hot coffee to my lips and take a sip, humming in approval as the contents warm my soul.

"Of course. Mila is out of town visiting her wicked bitch of a mother, so we have the room. And besides, what are friends for? Even if you left me high and dry at the bar last night. I came out of the restroom, and you were nowhere to be seen." Melissa snorts, clanking the coffeepot back on the burner a little harder than necessary.

"I'm so sorry, girl. You know that's totally unlike me. I never lose my head over a man." I groan, letting my head drop back and squeeze my eyes shut. Rubbing at them in hopes of ridding myself of his memory. It doesn't help. All I see are his rugged features, mocking me for not taking a chance.

I'm glad she's known me since high school. Yeah, I was two grades ahead of her and Mila, but us being the awkward outcasts had us bonding, nonetheless. And I know for a fact that she's never seen me act a fool over a man before, so at least she knows I'm telling the truth.

"Well, I guess it's about damn time. I just wish I could've seen him. The way you're describing him, sounds like he was a Greek god straight out of a textbook."

"Yeah, a Greek god that's totally off limits," I mumble into my coffee, still pouting over what I missed out on last night.

Melissa was pulling blueberries from the fridge, but my words have her halting her steps. "Hold up. Seems to me like that man was enamored, and based on what you're saying now, it seems like you might be as well. So pray tell, *why* couldn't you seal the deal?"

"My father."

Mel groans. "Why is that man behind every shitty thing in your life?"

"You know *why*. I owe him."

"No, you don't. You didn't put your mother in front of

that car. She chose to follow you. Yes, she chose to push you out of the way because she loved you that much. But that's what we do for the people we love. I know you would've done the same for her."

My nose stings and eyes prickle. It's so much more than that. If she only knew of the secrets I *now hide*. But I can't tell a soul. It's my fault and my burden to bear.

"I know what you're saying, Mel, but I can't help feeling guilty when I know it should've been me in front of that car, not her. I stripped that man of his partner, the woman he vowed forever to love. I'm a thief. A thief of joy and love. It's only fair I be denied the very thing I stole from him."

Mel scoffs. "As if that man ever loved a thing in his life. You and I both know that your mother was nothing more than a pawn in his game of chess."

Her words, though harsh, ring true. But I can't bring myself to admit them out loud. Maybe there's a part of me that longs for her to be wrong. That the fairytale version of my childhood wasn't something I'd constructed just to stay sane.

"Yeah, you're quiet because you know I'm speaking nothing but facts." She raises a brow as she pours some blueberries into her cereal. "Look, all I'm saying is you can't keep blaming yourself like this. That man is not your keeper, and you have to learn to forgive yourself if you ever want a chance at happiness in your life."

There she goes again, making sense. "Ugh, can't we

just drop it for now? Talk about you for a change? How's that broody mountain man you're always talking about?"

"My brother's best friend?" She rolls her eyes before shoving a spoonful of cereal into her mouth, mumbling, "Can't talk. Mouth full."

"Ha! I promise I won't pry if you drop this whole convo. Talking about it just makes me sad."

"No dice." Mel shakes her head. "I mean, I'll drop the Greek god, but I'm never giving up on getting through to you about you deserving happiness. That's no joke."

I awkwardly push my lips to the side and smile. "Thank you, friend. I appreciate you. I truly do."

"Back at ya, babe. So, now that the mushy stuff is out of the way, let's hatch a plan to free you from the evil clutches of your father." She twirls her spoon in the air while pursing her lips. "I'd say I'm pretty good at it. I helped Mila devise a plan to rid herself of her wicked bitch mother and now she lives here with me."

I laugh. "Yes, you're fantastic at planning, that's for sure. But I think I already have something in mind."

"Do tell." Mel waggles her brows in anticipation.

"Well, it's nothing concrete, but I've been scoping out this little storefront that's sat empty for some time now. I have some money saved up from working with Father and thought I'd branch out from just being one of his peons to a peon with a side hustle."

Mel's mouth drops open, her eyes fluttering like the wings of a hummingbird. "O-M-G! That's huge! You've always had an eye for fashion. Is that what the shop will be?"

I nod enthusiastically. "Yes! I've already been in contact with several vendors. Basically, I'd be the main point of sale for all the larger designers we typically have to drive into the city for. Sure, during the off-season we'll be business for mainly the locals, but in peak tourist season I'm sure all those visiting will appreciate my store."

Mel rushes over to me, placing one hand on each of my shoulders before lightly shaking me. "Girl, that's BRILLIANT! You already know I'll be your number one customer."

I smile, knowing she will be. "Now… to get that going without Father finding out, now that's a different story."

"*Screw him.* You don't owe him your soul, despite what's rolling around in that head of yours."

She's right. She *so* is, but no matter how much truth she speaks, it's as if that man holds a spell over me. And not the good kind, like my handsome stranger.

"Uh-oh. What's the reason for that glassy stare? I know the one. Happens to me every time I'm thinking of a particular mountain man." Mel gives my shoulder a shove, breaking me out of my daydream, the one where I'm waking up to muscular arms wrapped around me.

"Ugh, I can't help it. It's like he creeps up in my thoughts at will. Not even disparaging thoughts of my father could shake them."

"Ha!" Mel bellows. "Welcome to the club, sis. Looks

like you've been stung by the love bug. Good luck trying to get rid of it."

I purse my lips to the side. "Well, watch me do just that, because I have no other option."

Mel groans, lifting both hands in the air. "I give up. There's no hope for you, woman. This is a lesson you'll have to learn on your own. When the pain becomes too great, that's when you'll cave. You just watch."

Her words of wisdom try to sink in, but there's something inside of me that just won't let them take root. Maybe she's right. Maybe I just haven't suffered enough, the purgatory destined for me to be much greater.

On a sigh, I finally respond. "Time will tell."

Mel rolls her eyes, but smiles. "It sure will, and when it does, I'll be here to say *I told you so*."

Six Months Later

I look at the boxes in front of me and can't help but grin. My heart is soaring and I'm smiling so hard my dang cheeks hurt.

I've done it. I've actually done it.

I've set up my very own boutique, and even though it only operates on the weekends, it suits me just fine. Besides, the locals don't mind, and we still have some time until all the tourists make their way into our sleepy mountain town.

I'm taking the wins where I can, and right now it's in the form of this exclusive merch I just received.

I can't wait to call Mel. She's going to lose her mind! It's from her favorite designer, the one she's been begging me to carry in-store.

And speaking of the devil, I'm flipping open my box cutter, about to stab into the first box when I hear her call out my name.

"Hayley! You in here?" Her melodic tone drifts into the storage room, but something is off.

I rush to the front and stop dead in my tracks as soon as I spot her. "*What the fuck*? Girl! What happened to you?!" She's all black and blue, a fat lip, big enough to make Dolly Parton jealous.

My eyes immediately float to the mountain of a man behind her, his thick beard and menacing glare intimidating as hell, but so help me God if he's the one who's done this to her. "Do you need me to call the sheriff?"

Mel laughs, placing a hand on my shoulder to calm me. "I know I look scary, but Hunter didn't do this. Bruce did."

I suck in a sharp breath. "That bastard. I always knew he was no good, but I didn't think he'd ever hurt his own daughter."

Her dad is known for being a raging alcoholic around town, but he's never hurt so much as a fly—*or so I though*t.

She scoffs. "Well, looks like we were both wrong."

The looming stranger clears his throat, pulling my focus from Mel's battered face and back to his eerily familiar eyes. Studying his features further, it's almost as if I've seen him before. As if I've known him intimately. *But that's impossible.*

"We came here to get some things for Mel. You have things in her size, right?" He raises a bushy brow while staring me down, and I can't help but snort.

"Of course, I do. She's my best customer." Rolling my eyes, I walk past his lumbering frame to a new display area I've set up. "Get your butt over here, girl. I've got to show you what I just got in."

Mel rubs her hands together eagerly. "You don't have to tell me twice!"

I'm picking up a pair of boots when the chime above the door goes off, my eyes instantly darting toward it. *Holy shit. It can't be.*

"There you are. I've been looking for you everywhere." Matthew Crown, my handsome stranger is shaking his head at Mel's companion. I believe she called him Hunter.

"I told you. I needed to get my girl some things."

Okay. It seems like he's more than just her companion. *OMG, is this the mountain guy? Her brother's best friend?* She has some serious explaining to do. They're clearly together if he's claiming her like this.

My eyes are practically bugging out as I try to telepathically yell at Mel for keeping such a big secret from me, but her gaze is focused intently on her man. Her man. The one that seems to know Matthew Crown.

Well, I don't blame her. They're about the same height,

and the closer I look, the more similar they become. It's like they're carbon copies, but not. Where Matthew is polished sharp edges, Hunter is all scruffy and unkempt.

My handsome stranger speaks, and my heart picks up its pace. *I'm screwed.* Even his voice affects me. "Yeah, well, I thought you would make like every other normal person and head into the city." He chuckles but freezes mid laugh when his eyes finally fall on me.

Gaining a little bravado from his off-handed insult to my store, I speak up. "Normal is overrated." *He's just like my father.* A nay-sayer shitting on my dreams. Narrowing my eyes, I place my hands on my hips and give him a piece of my mind. "I'll have you know that I carry pieces that even the big city can't get their hands on."

Mel comes to my defense. "She has a point. I know. I've tried." She's nodding, her head bobbing up and down enthusiastically as her eyes bounce back and forth between Matthew and me. "Do you two know each other?"

"*No.*" I rush out just as Matthew utters, "Yes."

Well, so much for making that believable. The clear skepticism is written all over my friend's face.

Mel raises a brow and is about to say something when Matthew interrupts. "My bad. I must've mistaken you for someone else. *A thief.*"

The last two words are muttered under his breath, but I don't miss them, and they cut deep. *A thief.* Does he know? He couldn't.

"Mhm. Must've," I respond, staring him dead-on and refusing to cower.

Seconds pass in silence, but neither of us dare look away. It isn't until Mel is clapping her hands together that the tense moment finally breaks. "Alrighty then. Hayley, how about we let these two catch up and you can show me the new goods."

"Right. In fact, there's a new shipment out back. Why don't I show you?" I slap on the fakest smile I've ever delivered, but there's no way in hell I'm letting that man who called me a thief see me cower.

Yes. He might be right, and I might be a thief, but frankly, that has nothing to do with him and it's none of his damn business.

I'm paving the way toward the stockroom and away from the men—*thinking I'm in the clear*—when Mel starts in with her line of questioning. "Care to tell me what that was about?"

I don't even turn to look at her while I answer. "Nope."

"*Okay*. But I'm here if you ever need to vent. I know just how frustrating these Crown men can be."

Crown men. So they're related. Of course they are.

I chortle. "Yeah. Well, thank you, but I have nothing to say. You on the other hand, why is this Hunter guy calling you his girl?"

I'm thinking she'll need some more convincing and that turning the tables on her isn't going to work, but I'm wrong. Mel speed walks past me, bee-lining it toward an open box, her eyes going all teary. "Oh my god! We can talk about Hunter later. Is this what I think it is!?"

"Sure is, babe. Sure is." A big smile spreads across my face, and never have I been more thankful for the new Heidi Summers collection than I am now. Nothing like a good ol' fashioned distraction to get your friend off your back.

Chapter Five
MATTHEW

It's been months since I last laid eyes on my little thief and no matter how hard I try; I can't seem to keep her off my mind. She's always creeping up. Either in a wet dream that leaves me feeling like a damn teenager or when my brother mentions her in some off-handed remark about his girl.

Turns out the little siren is good friends with my soon to be sister-in-law. *Just my luck.*

As if I didn't already have a hard enough time keeping her off my mind, now I'll get to see her at every damn family gathering.

My stomach growls and I welcome the distraction. I didn't eat anything last night and my body is begging me for breakfast.

Food. Now.

I'm heading toward the kitchen when there's a knock at the door. It's five in the fucking morning. *Who in the hell is it?*

I pull my Sig Legion from its hiding spot and rack it, not taking any chances. With everything that's been going down in our family, I wouldn't put it past one of our enemies paying us a visit.

Peering out the privacy window, I let out a chuckle. *My fucking brother.* As soon as I've pulled the door open, Hunter is shoving a brown bag in my face.

"Breakfast tacos." He grumbles, walking straight past me.

I grab the bag quickly before it falls and unroll the top with deft fingers. "You're a damn saint. I was just about to make myself something."

Hunter snorts. "Brother, I'm far from a saint. Definitely not after what Mel and I did last night."

I roll my eyes, but don't miss the sick feeling of satisfaction that's plastered all over Hunter's face.

"Spare me the details. I get it. You finally got your head out of your ass and are blissfully in love." I take one of the tacos and unwrap the foil, taking a big bite as we enter the kitchen.

"No coffee?" Hunter's lip curls while staring at the empty coffeepot.

"Bro, it's five in the morning. I just woke up." I shove another bite of the delicious egg and cheese combo into my mouth before pointing at the cupboard right in front of him. "Feel free to make us some, though. And while you're at it, tell me why you're here. Don't get me wrong, I love spending time with you, but this isn't the norm."

Hunter mutters something before pulling down the pods and two mugs. "Catherine and Raul are still missing. Every time we get a lead on where they're staying, our intel is sabotaged or they move out before we can detain them."

Those slippery motherfuckers. "It wasn't enough for Catherine to fake a pregnancy and try to cheat Austin out of his inheritance, no, that bitch had to team up with our arch nemesis." I shake my head while raising a brow. "And you wonder why I have trust issues."

Hunter shoves a mug in my face. "We'll revisit your sudden disdain for women later, but right now we need to figure out how these assholes keep moving one step ahead."

"That's easy. *There's a mole.*"

"Another one? We've been so damn careful since we found out the kids' therapist was working with the cartel." Hunter scratches at his beard as he walks toward the massive window overlooking my land.

I'm nestled in thirty acres of Colorado mountain side and the view is nothing to sniffle at. Beautiful shades of pink and orange dance across the sky as the sun rises to greet us for the day.

"Sorry to burst your bubble of naivety but, don't you remember Catherine had us conned this whole time too? We just had her pegged as a gold-digger, not a gold-digger with higher aspirations and the ability to deceive even her own kin."

"You're right. Nobody is off-limits. Everyone is a suspect." He groans. "Why couldn't this shit be easy for once?"

"Ha! Life ain't easy. Thought you'd've learned that by now."

"Right again, brother. It isn't easy, and it seems to me a woman just taught you that lesson. Who is she? You've been tight-lipped and I've given you some time to breathe, but time's up. *Spill*."

I rub at my temples, wishing he'd just drop it already. "Lord. How'd I get so lucky to have this chatter box version of you while everyone else gets the stoic Hunter?"

"It's a twin thing, I guess. So, go on. Spit it out. Who's the girl?"

I suck in a long breath, debating whether I should finally come clean. After all, I endlessly teased Hunter about his mystery woman for ages. I guess the joke's on me.

"*Hayley*," I utter in one fell-swoop.

Hunter slowly turns from the window, his eyes narrowed and gaze assessing. "Hayley. *My Hayley*?"

Fire burns through me and I can't help the growl that rumbles in my chest. "She isn't *your* Hayley."

Hunter's lips spread into a wide grin. "Oh, this is good. This is *real* good. Seems to me like you've found the one." He's all smiles as he walks over to the table, plopping himself down in front of the greasy paper bag and pulling out a taco for himself. "You've even got the whole possessive caveman look going. Just like the rest of us."

I roll my eyes. "Don't know what you're talking about, brother. Hayley's a thief. Stole my wallet months ago and I haven't said as much as two words to her since running into her at that boutique."

"Well, you better get used to talking to her because she's in the wedding party and so are you." Hunter's brows furrow as he takes a sip of his coffee. "But hold up, what makes you think she stole your wallet? That girl's a damn angel. Haven't so much as heard her curse, let alone do something like steal."

I purse my lips and shake my head, thinking back to the time Radley said she'd called him a fuck-boy. Last I checked, *fuck* was a swear word. "Everyone's a suspect. Nobody is off limits. Remember, people can be deceiving. Maybe she's the damn mole."

Hunter snorts. "No way in hell, brother. We'd know by now. The girl practically lives in my cabin." He groans while grabbing at his genitals. "She's the reason I've got blue balls half the time. Mel won't fuck me if she's around, which is ALL THE DAMN TIME."

I raise a brow and smirk. "That doesn't seem to be a problem when her brother's around. From what I hear, you've traumatized the poor man on more than one occasion."

"What can I say? My girl's a bit of an exhibitionist." He shrugs while sighing. "Well, an exhibitionist around everyone except her best friend. Look, whatever floats her boat, I'm gonna do. That woman is pure gold and I'm keeping her kitty happy, and I don't give a flying fuck if the pope himself was watching."

I can't help but snicker. "She's got you whipped, brother."

"Just you wait. When you and Hayley get this all sorted, you're going to be one ass-whipped motherfucker, too."

This has me raising both brows. "Oh no. There'll be no such thing. I don't give a shit how tempting her lips are, or how inviting those legs become. There's no way on God's green earth that I'll ever willingly bed with a thief."

"Bro. I'm telling you. There must be some sort of misunderstanding. The Hayley I know would never steal a dime. She's too proud for that."

"Misunderstanding my ass. I know what happened because I lived it."

"And how did you come to live it? You never gave me the details of how this came about."

I abruptly rise from my chair and push away from the table. "Sorry, brother. I don't care to relive that stupid mistake any more than I have to. What happened happened and I'd die a happy man if I never have to think of it again."

Hunter raises both hands, palms exposed. "Fine. But let's get our asses to Jack's compound. We need to round-table about the mole."

"Compound? You mean ranch." I roll my eyes. "And I already told you who the mole is. It's Hayley. The thief."

"It's a fucking compound with all of the guards he has posted, and have you seen all of the security gear he's setup over the past year?" Hunter sighs while his head shakes side to side. "And *I* already told *you*. It isn't Hayley."

"Fine. But don't say I didn't warn you when her good girl facade falls off. And believe me, brother, *it will*."

Chapter Six
HAYLEY

"Help! Come into the office and say you have some sort of emergency. Anything will do. Just get me out of here!" I whisper-shout into the receiver, pleading for my life and hoping with all that I have that Mel comes to my rescue.

"I thought you said there wasn't anything going on between you and Matthew Crown." I can practically see her smug smile from here.

"Okay, so I might've withheld some information. But I promise to come clean as soon as you pick me up."

"Why can't you just leave? You have a car." I hear a

door open and close, some keys jangling in the background. Thank you, baby Jesus. I think she's on her way.

"You know why. Father."

"Ugh. That man. It's about damn time you told him to shove it where the sun don't shine."

"I will. One Day." I'm pacing back and forth, the cord of the office phone springing to its limits with each pass, but I can't stay still. Time isn't on my side. "Look, I promise, but right now Father's in the conference room with Matthew and I know he's about to try to reel me into his scheme. He's been trying to buy most of the shares in Tortured Crown whiskey, and I can't let Matthew think that I've been a part of his plan all this time."

A car door shuts and I hear the start of an engine before Mel sighs into the phone. "I just know there's so much more to this story and I'm not driving until you at least give me a little more."

I blow out a long breath, knowing I'll have to give her something.

"Fine. You remember that time at The Fox when I left without telling you?"

"Yeah, you said you'd been swept off your feet by— O.M.G. Was that Matthew? Is this why he was off limits? Yes! Yes, it is! You said it was because of Parker."

"Yes. It was him. And yes, he was off limits because of my father." I stop to lean my butt on the desk, needing something to ground me before I confess. "Father promised he'd give me the weekends off if I scoped out a restaurant for him. Said he needed the info to seduce the owner into letting him buy some of his business."

"Go on." Mel urges as the sound of a blinker goes off in the background. Good, at least she's on the move.

"I was meant to talk up the staff, schmooze and gather intel that would make Father's acquisition possible. The thought of it made me feel icky, but when you said you knew the bartender. I thought it was meant to be. Meant to have the weekends free so I could open up my boutique."

Mel lets out a long whistle. "Oh, Hayley. And you ended up seducing the very man instead of just the employees."

"I know. It looks so horrible." I groan, letting my back hit the top of my desk as I squeeze my eyes shut. "But at least I left. I didn't want him to think I slept with him just to try and get his business. I swear, as soon as I found out who he really was, I high tailed it out of there."

"And now, if he sees you working for Parker, he's going to think that the only reason you went to his house was because of your father." She sucks in a sharp breath just as I hear my office door jostle.

"Here you are, sweetheart." My father's syrupy sweet tone has me quickly sitting up with my butt still planted firmly on the desk.

Horror. Sheer horror sets in as I see Matthew standing there beside him, the menacing glare the most expressive feature on his soured face.

"Father. Did you need something?"

There's a snort, and I realize I must've placed the phone on speaker when I got up. *Oh no. Oh God, no.*

"Father. That's a stretch. That man hasn't been a father to you a day in his life." Mel mumbles, but it's obvious we've all heard her if Parker's face and Matthew's raised brows are any indication.

"Mel, um. I'll have to call you back."

"So I take it—" she responds, but I hit the end button before she can give anything else away.

I'm about to apologize when Matthew clears his throat. "Parker. You didn't tell me your daughter worked for you."

Ugh. He hates me. I know he does. He's not even looking at me and I can still feel the judgment in his eyes.

"Yes. She's officially been with me since she turned sixteen." Father looks between me and Matthew, his eyes slightly narrowing before he plasters a fake smile on his face. "You know, she's well versed in the business. In fact, she's the best in marketing."

Matthew clenches his jaw, the action making his chiseled cheekbones jump. "Is that so?"

"It's so. I was bringing you in here to show you some of the work she's done for our latest acquisition. Helped expand it overseas. And—"

Matthew raises a hand, palm faced toward my father, but his eyes never leave mine. "Enough. Tell you what, you let Hayley come work for me for three months, see what she can do for Tortured Crown, and if all goes well, I'll gladly fork over the shares you're seeking."

I suck in a sharp breath as my heart threatens to beat out of my chest. *That's absolutely ridiculous.* I'm about to object when my father's all too cheery voice cuts in.

"Ha! You've got yourself a deal."

I can't even bring myself to look at the man who just bargained me away as if I were some piece of cattle. No, my eyes are still laser focused on Matthew Crown. The man whose penetrating gaze hasn't budged since he uttered his demand.

I'm frozen. Paralyzed by the sheer heat in those big hazel orbs. I swear, it's as if he's devouring me whole, right in front of my father.

The thought sends a shiver through my body, and it doesn't go unnoticed by the handsome man before me. His eyes go straight to my chest, where my freaking nipples give me away every damn time.

My mind flashes back to the bar when he stared at them then, and I swore, with just one look it felt as if he'd licked them right then and there.

I'm panting, my chest rising and falling at the memory of my slit riding his fat girth. *God, it felt so good.*

"Hayley, sweetheart. Are you okay? You look flushed." Parker cuts into the moment, shaking me out of this lust induced haze.

Standing to my full five-foot-two, I attempt to clear my throat and smooth down my skirt. "Yes. Sorry. I hope I haven't caught anything." My eyes dash over to Matthew, who's now donning a smirk. *The jerk.* "It'd be a shame if I couldn't work under Mr. Crown because I've suddenly caught an illness."

The more I think about it, the better it sounds. But my plans of faking sick come to a screeching halt with Matthew's next words.

"I assure you, little doll, this deal won't happen without you working for Tortured Crown." His raised brow and his deep baritone voice are enough to send goosebumps erupting all over my flesh and the exchange doesn't go unnoticed by my opportunistic father.

"Of course, Mr. Crown." With a clap on Matthew's back and a glare sent my way, Parker gives him one hell of a reassurance. "My daughter will perform *any* task you give her."

My stomach churns as a sickening wave of shame moves through me. And my reaction to Father's words must be visible because Matthew's stare goes from heated to concerned in two-seconds flat, his head swiftly darting toward Parker and issuing what's nothing short of a threat.

"Listen, Mr. Barclay. I promise, here and now, that she'll never be disrespected; by me, my employees, or *anyone* else." His eyes are narrowed, lips pressing into a thin line.

I can't deny it. Seeing him like this. Staring my father down and putting him in his place… *it turns me on.*

Before I have the chance to get all flushed again, father cuts in, figuratively dousing me with a cold bucket of ice.

"Yes. Nobody dare disrespect *my daughter*." The last

two words are uttered with a slight tinge of disgust, and I wonder if Matthew can pick up on Parker's disdain.

"Good. So we have a deal." Matthew finally drops his death glare and turns toward the door, giving me his back. With one step forward, he commands over his shoulder. "Nine o'clock Monday morning. Don't be late."

A lump forms in my throat, and it goes nowhere despite my swallow. All I can do is nod because words fail me.

No matter. He doesn't wait for a response. Matthew Crown, my handsome stranger, walks into the hall and out of my office, leaving me staring at empty space in his wake. Well, that's until Parker closes the door.

"Care to tell me what that was all about?" He's raising a brow as his tall frame closes in on me. "It's almost as if you two knew each other."

Deny, deny, deny. "I don't know what you're talking about. Never met him before."

My stomach churns as I speak. *Ugh.* I don't like lying and this feels absolutely horrible. Even if it's for a good cause. There's no way I'll let Parker hold that chance encounter over Matthew's head. *No.* Over my dead body.

I'm trying to get off of the desk, but Father's proximity is making it difficult. And as if that weren't enough, he makes it physically impossible when he reaches up and tightly grips my jaw, his brute strength keeping me in place.

"Listen here, child. You will do everything that man asks of you. And I do mean everything. I don't care what virtuous implications he may have given just now. He's a man. A man who clearly liked what he saw." His hold on my face tightens and I can't hold back the whimper. "You owe a debt, and this will be your payment. Seduce him if you have to. Do whatever it takes. But come back without securing those shares and I can assure you—the hell you've endured these past four years will be nothing compared to the hell you'll face. Got it?"

My eyes burn as hot tears trickle down my cheeks. This man is vile. Pure evil. I will never give him what he wants. Even now, as his nails dig into my flesh, the biting sting of the tips piercing through skin, I don't speak. Won't even let a whimper escape.

"Doesn't matter." He sinks his nails in further and I know he's drawn blood. "Bob your head and show me you understand." Against my will, he moves my head up and down like a mannequin, and a wicked smile dances across his lips. "There you go. Bout time you earned your keep."

He snivels, his nose wrinkling before he's pushing me so hard I have to brace my hands on the desk. "Go home, Hayley, and take care of this." He waves a hand in my direction. "Groom whatever it is that needs grooming and pick out your sluttiest office attire. You're getting me those shares."

I'm stunned silent as I watch my father's back disappear into the hall. Yes, he's always been demanding, cold and detached, but he's never asked this of me. Never bartered me off like cattle in exchange for profit.

How could he do this? It doesn't matter. *I can't... I just can't.*

Running toward the wastebasket, I let myself collapse, dry heaving into the black can and praying that I can throw up every bit of ick I feel inside.

My throat is raw and hot tears stream down my face, but nothing comes. This sick sensation remains.

This is just too far. I don't care what hell that man puts me through. The devil himself could threaten to drag me to hell, but I will never lie to Matthew, and *I will never sell my soul.*

Chapter Seven
MATTHEW

"Brother, all I'm saying is if I get word of you making that girl cry, there'll be hell to pay." Hunter presses his knuckles onto my desk, attempting to mean mug me into letting Hayley off the hook.

No can do.

"I'm doing this for the family. What better way to uncover her being the mole than by letting her work for me? I can watch her every move and there'll be no way of hiding her true colors."

"You're delusional. There's no helping you." Hunter stands tall, the calloused tips of his fingers rubbing at his temples. "Look. All I know is that if I have to end up catching shit from Mel, you're living that hell right along with me."

I grin, bearing my pearly whites while holding up both hands, palms exposed. "Oh no. You're the one who wanted to be in a relationship. I've steered clear of that nonsense, so you're on your own, brother."

At this, Hunter snorts. "You're so in the thick of it you don't even see it. The guys and I all have a bet going. *How long till Matthew drops.* I say a week, tops. You won't be able to resist her pull having her work right under you."

I roll my eyes at his certainty. "You're being ridiculous. Of course I can. She's a thief. And she won't just be working under me, she's coming to stay at my house."

Hunter's jaw drops open as his eyes practically bug out. "What the fuck?! Mel didn't tell me this."

"That's because the little thief doesn't even know it yet." I rub at my scruff, the rasping sound giving texture to the silent pause. "I intend to be on her ass twenty-four-seven. She won't be able to so much as sneeze without my knowing it."

I didn't have cameras on her the night we met at The Fox, but you bet your ass I won't be making that same mistake again.

Hunter's lip curls and brows drop. "Isn't that a little *excessive?*"

I wave his question away. "How else am I supposed to prove she's the mole? Anyone could put up a front for eight hours a day, but they sure as hell can't for an entire twenty-four hours."

"I don't think that's accurate. I'm pretty sure there are career criminals who'll disagree with you."

"See, that's the type of negativity that's kept you blind all this time." I get up and walk to the attached bathroom, stopping at the door frame before turning to look back. "But don't worry, brother. Hayley is on her way up here and it's a good thing I have enough insight for the both of us. You'll see. I'll be proven right."

A beat passes before Hunter is snickering under his breath and I have to turn once again, but this time from my vantage point in front of the mirror.

"Yeah. Okay, Matthew. You've got 20/20 vision on this."

"Of course I do." My nose turns up and eyes narrow, unsure of what he finds so fucking funny.

"Right. That's why you're checking yourself out like some teenage boy, fussing with that blazer and those fitted slacks. And I'm sure that you're donning this ensemble today because you have some other important meeting, not just Hayley, right?"

My chest squeezes and—*holy fuck*—maybe he's onto something. My normal office attire consists of a button-up, jeans, and a pair of my Lucchese boots—*not a full-on monkey suit.*

I'm not given much time to ponder the meaning of this because there's a knock at the door. *It's her.*

"Come in." I walk a few steps, clearing the bathroom threshold just in time to see a pair of slender legs enter my office.

She's a fucking vision, and it takes all that I have to not visibly react. I can already see my brother's smirk, and I'm not even looking at him. No. My eyes are focused on an angel in white. Surely a subliminal tactic, throwing me off and implying purity when she's anything but.

"Hunter?" Hayley's eyes dart to my brother and then back to me, where they belong. That's right, sweetheart. I see how my presence affects you.

Her neckline reaches just below her collar, and just like the other times I've seen her, it does nothing to hide the gorgeous tits below. Yes, her dress is demure and understated, but her body still betrays her, and those hard little nipples give her away.

I'm full-on ogling her when Hunter's chuckle shakes me out of my intense stare. "Make that a day, tops."

"What?" Hayley's innocent tone has my blood pressure rising. How dare she act clueless when she damn well knows what's going on here.

"Nothing. My brother is being an ass. An ass who was just leaving."

At this, Hunter raises a brow. When he opens his mouth to say something, I cut him off, placing a hand on his upper back and practically shoving him out of the room.

"Not a fucking word." I whisper behind him before

giving him a last push into the hall and closing the door behind him.

"Is..is everything okay?" Her voice shakes a little and I instantly feel like an ass.

Taking in a centering breath, I let myself turn toward her, slowly assessing the beauty before me. I can't let myself get lost in this girl. No matter how breathtaking she is.

She may put up a good front, acting all innocent, but I know who she truly is. "Everything is fine, Ms. Barclay." I gesture toward the loveseat against the wall, not moving an inch until that tight little ass of hers is sitting down right where I want it. "Did Rosie offer you a coffee?"

She blinks up at me from her seat and I swear those are the prettiest damn eyes I've ever seen. *Enough.*

"Yes, she did, but I declined." She pulls at the hem of her dress, the length hitting just below her knees. "I have to pee a lot when I'm nervous and I didn't think it'd be a good idea seeing as how I didn't know what we're going to be doing today. I didn't know if I'd be near a restroom and I didn't want to put you out if we'd have to make a million stops, you know? My job is to promote your business, not make you a babysitter to someone with possible incontinence issues."

My brows push together as I take in her incessant but adorable ramble. *Is she really nervous, or is this just another part of the act?*

Either way, her flushed cheeks and inability to meet my

gaze make me ache for her. The thought of her discomfort makes me so damn sick. Even if its feigned.

Needing to bring her comfort, I lower myself next to her and do something I know I shouldn't.

I take her hand in mine and instantly regret it.

Like a bolt of lightning, there's a current that passes between us and I know she feels it too. Her eyes quickly dart up to mine, those chocolaty orbs as big as saucers, are a huge indicator. And if I needed more of a tell, her pillowy lips part and she's sucking in sharp bursts of air, the action making her full tits heave right in front of me —the fuckers teasing me, begging me to have a little taste.

Focus, Matthew.

"Listen here, doll. Everything is okay. Everything is going to be okay." I let my thumb stroke the delicate skin of her hand and watch her bottom lip tremble in response.

"Okay," she whispers before taking in a deep breath, and for the first time since meeting her, I wonder if maybe this isn't all an act. Maybe she really is this anxious.

Hard to fake what looked like the onset of a panic attack. Well, time will tell. For now, I have to keep my guard up. For my family's sake.

"Alright then. Glad that's cleared up." Quickly shooting up from the loveseat, I turn back to tower over her, needing to issue a reminder. "Just know this, little one. That promise holds true just as long as you don't fuck over my family. Because if you ever do—"

She holds up a tiny palm that practically pushes me away. "Say less. It's understood."

The small sass-pot stands up, meeting me toe-to-toe, her gaze lifting to meet my own in defiance. "Now that that's been cleared up, what's the first thing on the agenda, boss?"

Well, slap my ass and call me Sally. Who's this little spitfire that's a complete one-eighty from the girl I comforted on the couch?

Ha! I think I've been right all along, and I'm going to have one hell of a time proving it.

Hayley

My eyes narrow into tiny slits as I stare at him head on. Well, more like head to chest, he's so dang tall.

How dare he?! This man really thinks me capable of hurting his family. That warning really wasn't necessary, and to be honest, it was quite hurtful.

I guess I can't really blame him with how I bailed on him the last time we were alone. My mind flashes back to the night where our bodies were pressed up against each other so intimately, and I can't help but blush.

Damn it to hell.

I wear my heart on my sleeve and the pompous ass is smirking at me now, no doubt reading me like a book.

"First on the agenda is taking a tour of the facility. Then

you'll meet with the team to get a feel of who and what you're promoting." He turns to walk toward his desk and the view I'm greeted with is absolutely delicious. The fitted blazer shows off the broad V of his back, tapering down to what could only be described as buns of steel, lifting and clenching with every step in those slacks.

"Hayley… eyes up here." The smug bastard is grinning now as I drag my eyes to his and meet his backward stare.

Of course he'd catch me ogling him. Geez. Get it together, girl.

"So are we starting this tour or what?" My new *Modus Operandi*—admit nothing and change the subject.

He chuckles, but thankfully doesn't tease me further. Instead, he sits behind his desk and types something out before returning his attention to me. "Yes, it'll have to be quick, but I want you to get a feel for the company. It isn't just a distillery, it's like an extended family and I firmly believe that's part of what makes the whiskey so good."

I smile at that. The idea of each bottle being infused with the warmth and love he so clearly has for his brand. "I like that. Definitely something we should include in the marketing angle."

"Good. I agree." He raises a brow as he pulls a set of keys out of a desk drawer, his thick fingers playing with a metal keychain resembling a fox. "Once we're done with that, we'll drive over to your place and pick up your things."

This has my eyes darting from his hand up to his face,

my own brows scrunching together in confusion. "I'm sorry, what? Did you just say we're going to my place?"

My heart is beating a mile a minute at the idea of having him where I sleep, bathe, and eat. That's way too intimate. I need to keep my distance if I have any hope of surviving the next three months.

It's clear my body reacts to his and I *in no way* can cave to my father's demands. I *cannot* be intimate with this man.

"That's right." He walks toward me, eliminating the space between us and leaving his towering frame mere inches apart. "It's my understanding you live a good two hours away from here. Makes no sense for you to make that commute every single day when I have a perfectly good spare room in my home." He pauses, eyes narrowing and assessing as he delivers another underhanded insult. "It's spacious, but I don't need to remind you. I'm sure you remember it well."

My face flushes once more, but this time from a mixture of indignation and anger.

Yes, I might have left without saying goodbye, but I wasn't *ghosting* him.

"Look, it's best we get this out of the way." Refusing to let him make me feel bad, I close whatever gap there was between us and practically step on his toes. "I'm sorry if I hurt your fragile male ego, but it wasn't anything personal. *Trust me*. I was doing you a favor."

At this he scoffs, his chest coming millimeters from my nose. "Little doll. You did not hurt my ego. I know who I am and what I have to offer." There's a pause as he stares me down, and a glimmer of something flashes behind his eyes, but I don't have time to assess what it is because his next words leave me dumbfounded. "No, you didn't hurt me, but what you did is much worse. You took from me, and that is something I will never forget."

I'm stumbling back, my mouth hanging open as I try to gather my thoughts. *Took from him? What is he talking about?*

"I have no idea—" I'm cut off mid-sentence with a knock at the door followed by Rosie entering the room.

"Rosie, thank you." Matthew takes the to-go cup from her hands before he's shoving it in mine. "Here. I emailed Rosie. One cream, two sugar."

My brows furrow and nose scrunches as I look down at the warm cup. "What's this?"

I'm still staring down at it as if it were a foreign object when he responds. "It's coffee. One cream, two sugar." I'm about to go into my whole needing to pee spiel again when he holds up a hand. "Don't worry. You can stop as many times as you need to."

How? How is this man both considerate and rude? It's like he's Jekyll and Hyde.

My face is still scrunched with confusion, but I offer my gratitude anyway. "*Okay*... Thank you?"

"Alright then. Rosie, is Sara ready to take her on that tour?" Matthew looks to his secretary while I'm still a jumble of thoughts and questions.

"Yes, sir. She's right outside." Rosie gestures toward the door, her warm smile extended toward me. "Whenever you're ready Ms. Barclay."

I give her a tight-lipped nod as I walk to the door and away from the handsome stranger who is a stranger no more. Nope. He's an enigma, one I can't afford to explore.

I've managed to clear the threshold when his deep voice almost causes me to stumble, "Have her back by noon, we've got quite the drive ahead of us."

Oh, quite the drive it'll be.

Chapter Eight
HAYLEY

"Hayley, meet Sara. She's the admin overseeing the boys in logistics. Knows this place like the back of her hand. And that's exactly why *she'll* be giving you the grand tour today." Rosie smiles at the brunette, but it feels forced. *Interesting.* I wonder if there's bad blood between the two. "That said, I'll be right here if you need anything. You just holler."

I lift the coffee cup in gratitude and offer her a smile. "Thank you, Rosie. I appreciate it. You've been so kind. And this coffee, it's perfect."

"Yes, she makes the best coffee, doesn't she?" Sara cuts in, bringing my attention back to her.

I'm trying not to stare at my tour guide, but her six-inch stilettos and super short dress make it nearly impossible to drag my gaze away. Yes, I'm all about fashion. After all, it's what I live for. But given the setting, her attire seems a *little* much.

"That she does." I force my eyes back to meet her steely blue and take a sip of the delicious concoction. *It's perfec*t. Just the way I take it.

How did Matthew know?

"Hatley, was it?" Sara's question breaks me out of my thoughts. She's smirking, all the while guiding me toward the building's exit.

I may be a pushover with my father, but hell will freeze over before I give anyone else that privilege. So with the fire in my belly, I set this girl straight.

"No. It's *Hayley*." I stand my ground, refusing to move an inch until she's acknowledged what I've said.

"Right. *Hatley*." Her smirk deepens and eyes narrow as she opens the door outside before stepping into the blazing Colorado sun. "I'm not sure how much experience you have working with a distillery, so I'll start with the basics. This—"

Enough. I interrupt her condescending lecture and lift a hand, effectively propping the door open and preventing it from shutting in my face. "Sara, I don't know what problem you have with me or what preconceived notion might lurk in that head, but I assure you, I've come here with no ill will and I'd appreciate it if you cut the attitude." Her mouth goes from tightly curled up to slightly agape. But I'm not done. "Once more, it's *Hayley*. Not Hatley."

"Okay, Hayley." She clears her throat and straightens the front of her skirt. "I've been working here for over a year now. I'm the only woman on the team besides Rosie, and I intend on it staying that way." She purses her lips, but I'm not interrupting her very telling rant. "It's my understanding that you're only going to be here for three months, and it's my job to help you learn as much as possible about our growing business. The way I see it, the faster I get this information across, the faster you'll do your job and be gone. So, if you're done lecturing me about the correct pronunciation of your name, and if it's alright with you, Princess Hayley, may we move on with this tour?"

The freaking audacity! I wasn't complaining about the pronunciation. She was outright calling me by a different name, and she knows it.

This gaslighting little bi—

"Ladies. Everything okay?" Matthews' deep voice reverberates behind me, and I can't help the goosebumps it elicits.

And it seems like I'm not the only one it affects.

"Mattie! I didn't see you standing there." Sara, who'd been the epitome of cold and calculating, turns into a fawning mess. "Is there anything I can get you? I know Rosie already got you your morning coffee, but maybe I can fetch you a donut from the warehouse? The boys brought them over from Poppy's."

Matt's brows raise. "That's very tempting, but there's no need to fetch me anything, Sara. I've already told you. That's not your job."

Sara's cheeks turn a heated pink as her gaze drops to the ground. *Who is this woman and where is the viper that was ready to claw my eyes out minutes ago?*

"I know, Mattie. I just like taking care of you."

Ahh. I get it. She has the hots for the boss.

Immediately, I'm sucker punched in the gut with something I've never felt before. It's this gnawing feeling of uneasiness, and now I'm the one wanting to claw Sara's eyes out.

I suck in a sharp breath as it dawns on me. *I'm jealous.* And unfortunately for me, my gasp draws everyone's attention and now I have both sets of eyes facing my direction.

"You okay, doll?" Matthew places a hand on my back, and I can't hide the shiver that runs through me.

I swallow thickly, but can't respond because Sara cuts me off.

"Of course she's fine. She's probably just a little overwhelmed." Sara attempts to playfully knock his hand off my back, but this man is a brick wall, and I don't think Samson himself could pry him off.

"Sara, I appreciate your trying to help, but I'll take over from here. Thank you." All warmth that'd been in his tone evaporates and he's staring her down as if she were a complete stranger. I almost feel bad for her. *Almost.*

"But Mattie. I've got it covered. Surely you have more important things to do." Sara bats her lashes and attempts a pout that ends up looking more like duck lips. *Wow.* She's trying hard. "The boys said Spence was looking for you this morning. Let me help with this teensy little thing."

She places a palm on his biceps; her manicured nails scratching slighting with those last three words. It makes me want to scream! *What in the heck is wrong with me?*

"Did they say what the sheriff was after?" Matthew asks, bringing my attention to his face. He's staring at me intently, despite his question being directed at Sara.

And speaking of, her hand travels higher toward his shoulder as she answers his question. "Didn't say, but I'm sure he'll tell you when you call."

My eyes are zeroed in on her hand as it attempts to make its way to his muscular traps. Those things must look amazing under that shirt because their outline right here and now are drool worthy on their own. *How much longer is she going to fondle him?*

There's a chuckle, and—*thank you, Lord*—Matthew takes a step back, the action causing Sara's hand to drop. I finally let out a breath I didn't know I was holding and meet my boss's gaze once more.

"No, thank you, Sara." Matthew raises a brow, his hand dropping to my lower back as his thumb gives me a slight caress. "I've got this handled."

"But the sheriff? He—" she starts to whine but Matthew cuts her off.

"I said I have it handled, Sara. Now, if you'll excuse us, we have to make this quick. It's a long drive to Ms. Barclay's apartment."

I'm not sure why he's mentioned our little road trip, but I'm secretly glad that he did.

Sara's face is positively fuming and I'm internally doing a little jig. *Fuck that bitch.* OMG! I feel my eyes widen in horror. *Who am I becoming?*

I've never in my life cursed like this, nor have I ever felt such intense sensations of rage toward someone who's never actually harmed me. *This is all Matthew; it has to be.*

"Come now, doll. We've got a lot to cover and not a lot of time." Matthew presses me forward, and like a good little girl I comply, my feet walking in the direction he's suggested.

"Why do you call me 'doll'?" I'm speaking before thinking, and I realize that this is in no way professional.

Well, neither is his hand on my body, yet here we are.

"Hadn't realized that I was." Matthew's brows furrow as we stop in front of a massive red barn.

He drops his hand to open a small door leading us inside, and I'm left bereft of his touch. But I'm not given much time to wallow in the loss because the vision before me is stunning.

Wow. This is amazing. Massive wooden vats fill the

room and the aroma of whiskey in its infancy hits me full-force.

"This is where it all begins. Malting raw grain until it's just right and ready to move on to the next phase." His eyes glisten as he looks at all the barley resembling porridge. You can feel the pride he takes in his work, and it's absolutely beautiful.

"Is it true that you don't use any computers?" I ask, effectively bringing his gaze back toward me, and the surprise I see in them is clear in the raising of his brows.

"So you've researched the company, have you?"

"Of course. I'm the best at what I do for a reason." I place a hand on his forearm and feel the instant jolt, but keep it there just the same. "It's my job to make your baby shine, helping it grow and become the best version of itself. Not turn it into something else."

His full lips part and my mind immediately wonders what they'd taste like.

"I'm glad you've said that, Hayley, because that has been one of my biggest concerns with selling these shares to your father."

Right. My father. That's why you're here, not because of his damn lips. *Geez Louise. Get it together.* I swear you'd think I've never been around a handsome man before.

Finally removing my hand, I clear my throat. "Well, I give you my word. I will do no such thing. Besides, you get final say in any marketing campaign I engage in."

He purses his lips and slowly nods. "Your word. You give me your word."

My nose scrunches and brows furrow. "Yes, my word."

I don't know what happened, but his face loses all trace of emotion. It's as if he's turned it off at the spigot.

"Once we're through with the malting, we move on to mashing in order to pull the sugars from the grain."

I simply nod, even though I'm very familiar with how whiskey is made. It's been my father's obsession for as long as I can recall, and I suppose a part of me thought that if maybe—just maybe—I learned enough about it, that he'd finally accept me as his own.

"From there, we move on to the fermentation process." We walk toward the back of the room where large vats sit and the distinct aroma of yeast floats in the air.

"Boss!" Someone hollers, and I turn to see a young man in his early twenties stopping dead in his tracks as soon as he spots us. "Sara's rolled her ankle real bad."

I snort. *I can't freaking help it.* Of course she'd roll her ankle right as 'Mattie' gives me a personal tour. That girl is a pro walking in those heels, and I bet if push comes to shove, she could even run in them things.

Thankfully, both men ignore me and Matthew answers while rubbing at his temples. "Is she okay, or does she need to see the doc?"

"Looks like she needs the doc because of how hard she's crying. You'd think her foot snapped right off." His brows raise as he shakes his head in disbelief. "We've told her not to wear those things. They're a safety hazard."

Now I snicker. I thought the same thing. But unlike before, this sound garners their attention.

"I'm sorry. Didn't mean to interrupt, boss. Just needed to know if you were okay with one of us taking her to see Doc Johnson." His lips push to the side as he rubs at his scruff. "She'd asked for you personally, but a couple of the men offered, seeing as how you're always so busy."

Of course she asked for him. I roll my eyes and catch Matthew staring at me again, a slow smile spreading across his lips.

"Thank you for looking out, Andrew. Yes, please have one of the men take her. Put it all on the company card and keep me posted with what the doc says." Matthew hands him a black metal card, but his eyes never leave me. "And Andrew, this is Hayley. She'll be with us for the next three months. Make sure to tell the other men she's not to be bothered."

This has my head rearing back and brows pushing together. "It's really no big deal if someone needs my help with something."

I try to assure them both, but Matthew isn't having it. "You are here to help with marketing and marketing alone." His jaw tightens as his eyes drift to poor Andrew, and I swear his employee looks just as confused as I feel. "Please let the men know that if they have any concerns about Ms. Barclay, they are to direct them toward me. Got it?"

Andrew's brows raise as he nods and a slow smile spreads across his lips. "Got it, sir. The girl is off-limits." He winks, before sparing me a quick glance. "I'll let the boys know the wolf is on the prowl."

This earns him a frustrated grunt from Matthew. "Just do what I say. Nothing more. Nothing less."

It's clear his employees feel comfortable with him because Andrew chuckles before bellowing over his shoulder. "Sure thing, boss! You have fun now, and holler if you need anything."

Matthew groans as Andrew steps behind a giant vat before disappearing outside. "Don't mind him. They're all like family and think they can get away with saying stupid shit like that."

I giggle. "It's okay. I think it's endearing how much your employees feel comfortable with you. It says a lot about you as a boss."

His face turns the slightest tinge of pink and I do believe the stoic Matthew Crown is blushing!

"Like I've said, this is so much more than a business."

I nod, offering this handsome man a small smile. "It shows."

We stand there, staring at each other with eyes slightly narrowed. There is so much to be said but neither of us dare speak.

It isn't until the hissing of a machine in the distance breaks the spell and Matthew carries on once more. "Okay, then. Let me show you our stills."

He brushes past me, leading the way out, and so help me God, I can't avoid looking at his ass. It's perfect and should come with a work hazard sign. *Gah.* I'm supposed to keep this strictly professional—in direct opposition to what my father wants—but at this rate, I'm cruising for nothing but disappointment.

I can't afford a misstep. *I just can't.* So grasping at what little self-restraint I still possess, I drag my eyes away and focus on the laundry list of things I need to do in order to make his company more successful.

I may not be able to have the man, but at least I'll leave a mark on something he loves so dearly.

Chapter Nine
MATTHEW

"Get in." I hold the door to my blacked-out truck and wait for the pint-sized doll to climb in, but instead I'm met with a look of apprehension.

"First, I never agreed to come live with you for three months. And second, how in the world am I supposed to get up into that thing?"

"Like this." Taking the opportunity when I see it, I grip both hands around her waist and hoist her inside, making sure to reach over and buckle her in tight.

She's left sputtering but doesn't complain, so I playfully flash her a smirk before shutting the door and walking over to the driver's side.

"This isn't up for negotiation, doll. There aren't any rentals in the area and I'm not having you drive four hours every damn day." I see that she's about to protest, so I interrupt her mid-complaint. "Look, it isn't safe and I'll be stressin' every minute you're out on those roads."

"*You're* worried about *me?*" There's a mixture of wonder and disbelief in her tone, and I'm left wondering if anyone's truly worried about her before.

"Yes." I reply without thinking because it's true. Even though I think her a thief and a liar, there's something about her that calls to me. It's this bizarre need to protect her and keep her safe. Bizarre, because the very reason I have her here is to prove her the rat she is, and safe is the last thing she'll be when my brothers find out exactly what she's capable of.

Oblivious to my inner dialogue, she fidgets with the hem of her dress, the position she's in making the cream fabric ride up and expose the curve of her knees and slender thighs. My cock twitches at the sight and I have to remind myself that she's completely off-limits. Not just to the men at the distillery, but to me as well.

She's trouble, any way you look at it. Temptation on a stick, sent to take me straight to Hell. From those fuckable lips to that luscious ass meant to take a pounding. *Fucking sinful.*

"Eyes up here." The little brat smirks, feeding me the

very words I'd uttered this morning. *Touché.* "You'll want to get on I-70, then. It's the fastest way to my place."

"I know," is all I say as I start the car. I know this earns me a raised brow, but I'm not giving her any answers. Let's just say she isn't the only one who's done research.

"Right. You probably looked up the paperwork Rosie had me fill out." She nods, speaking more to herself than to me.

Whatever you think, doll. There I go again, calling her by that pet name. Maybe there's some truth to what my brother was saying. I like her. Let's face it. I don't ever think I stopped liking her. Not even when I found out what she was really capable of.

Either way—like her or not—I can't get attached. I have a mission and I will not stray.

Hayley sighs just then, letting her head fall back on the rest and fluttering her eyes closed. *Fuck, she's perfect.* Scanning the contours of her face, I realize they're nothing short of divine.

Oh, hell. This shit isn't going to work. Not if I can't even look at her without being in awe. My fingers curl tightly around the steering wheel as we roll into the interstate, and I come face to face with my predicament.

I need to set up boundaries—something, anything, if I'm going to make it out of this unscathed.

"Only pack the bare minimum. Remember, you aren't really moving in so there's no need to bring your entire apartment with you." I feel disgust at what I've just said, and if I were being truly honest, a part of me wants to do just that—pack up her entire apartment and move her in with me.

Thank God Hayley quickly brings me to my senses with her next words, my temporary insanity a thing of the past.

"Move in with you? Ha! You haven't even gotten me to agree with the short stay!" She's turned her small body toward me now and is attempting to stare daggers into my soul. *It's fucking adorable.*

This pint-sized fiery bundle is getting redder by the minute as she sees the glee in my eyes, and I can't help but chuckle.

"Baby doll, you're *mine*." My cock fills as soon as the words are out, and I realize just how much I wish they were true. Reaching down, I adjust my girth, all the while staring the little spitfire dead in the eye. "For the next three months, you're *my responsibility*. That means everything about you is my concern. I will feed you, clothe you, and keep you safe. Anything that little mouth of yours needs, I'll provide. Is that clear?"

Hayley licks her lips, her gaze glued to where my hand rests. *That's right, baby. You did this.*

As if reading my mind, her cheeks turn pink and eyes flash up to mine. I'm met with hunger hiding behind those chocolate orbs and I'd be lying if I said I didn't like it.

"You know you don't have to do all that. You aren't my *daddy*."

Jesus, Mary, and Joseph. Visions of taking this girl over my lap, slapping that tight ass and having her beg for Daddy—it all has cum dribbling out of my steely shaft and the need to impale myself in her hot little cunt intensifies tenfold.

What-the-actual-fuck? And because I've apparently lost my mind, I'm talking before I can think better of it.

"Well, seems to me like maybe that's what you need. A daddy." My eyes are on the road, but I don't miss her sharp intake of air.

I thought my cock had reached its limit, but I swear it grows another inch with her next words.

"And you want to take on that role? You want to be my... *daddy*?"

Yup. Whatever this is, there's no stopping it. Hearing that one little word come out of her mouth has turned me into a savage, needing to take and stake my claim. There's a burning need to show her what it's like to truly be cherished and adored. All the while shoving myself so deep in her, she has no option but to know she's mine.

Needing her to know just how serious I am, I pull out into the shoulder, letting other cars zoom by. *Fuck them and fuck the boundaries.* This is important.

Once I've placed the truck in park, I turn to face my one true weakness. This girl. This fallen angel that's been sent to test my will.

"Matthew?" Her chest is rising and falling quickly now,

teasing me with those perky tits as the evidence of her excitement urges me on.

"No, doll. I'm Daddy as far as you're concerned." With one hand, I grip her pretty little throat and apply the slightest bit of pressure. "But know this. If I ever find out you've misbehaved, you *will* be punished." I let my thumb caress the elegant column of her neck, feeling the rapid beat of her pulse intensify with every stroke. "And, baby, my spanking that round little ass will be the least of your worries."

Hayley lets out a whimper before she's licking her luscious lips and I swear I just about cum in my pants. *God*, I'm painfully hard, but this isn't the time nor place for relief. First, I need to know she's on the same page.

"*Come.*" In one swift move, I lift her from her seat and drag her to me, hiking up her dress and making her straddle me. *Fucking heaven.* Her sweetness settles right over my hard length, and I can't hold back the moan it elicits.

Hayley gasps, her brows raising as her entire body flushes. "*Oh, wow.*"

"Don't look so shocked, doll. Your hot little cunt's rubbed all over this cock before, and if I recall correctly. You loved every second of it. What do you say, baby? If I touched you now, like I did then, would your pussy weep for me? Would it weep with the need to have me shove myself deep inside it?"

Hayley doesn't verbally answer, but the biting of her fat

bottom lip and the slow seductive roll of her slit along my hard ridge tells me all I need to know.

Christ. I'm so ready to fill her, bouncing that tight little cunt on my cock until she's screaming my name. But I can't. Not now. Not until she truly understands what she's getting herself into.

"You are mine. Mine to cherish and mine to punish." I pull her forward just a tad and demand an answer. "Now, be a good girl and tell Daddy you understand."

Hayley's lips part as she shivers under my grip, goosebumps erupting all over her pretty flesh. This angel is just about to speak when the fucking buzzing of a cell phone cuts into the moment and my damn truck announces an incoming call.

"Spencer Brown." A disembodied voice rings through the cabin, "Incoming Call from Spencer Brown."

Of course, that asshole would call right now. Begrudgingly, I move Hayley back to her seat but raise a brow in warning, "This isn't over."

This earns me a scoff. "It sure is, *Daddy*. And for the record, I haven't agreed to any of this."

The little brat smirks, thinking she's off the hook. *Think again.*

Reaching over, I hike up the remaining fabric of her dress before inserting two fingers down the hem of her panties and find what I'd been looking for.

She's slick with need and I take full advantage, running

a finger down her slit and coating it with her juice, rubbing at her little pearl while her body arches for me.

"Say what you want, doll, but your wet little cunt is telling me otherwise."

She's gasping, but her legs are opening up, giving me a wide berth to play. Unfortunately for us, Spencer keeps calling.

"Matthew," my girl is mewling as I keep tweaking that hard little button and I have no doubt that if I keep playing with it, she'll unravel for me like the sweetest flower.

"Soon, baby. I promise." I push in just the tip of my finger, teasing her, letting her know I'm far from done. "But I don't share, and these sounds you're making? They're just for Daddy."

I give her cunt a quick little slap, enjoying her gasp turned moan.

"Incoming call from—" The voice starts again. *Fucking hell.* This better be good.

"Talk Spence. What'd you got for me?" I take the call off speaker and pull the cell phone to my ear. I don't care how hot Hayley is, or how gorgeous her pouty lips would look wrapped around my cock—*I still don't trust her.*

"You are one hard man to get a hold of." He bitches and I just don't give a damn.

"Right. Well, you got me on the line now, so what's good?"

"It's the Feds, man. They're breathing down my neck for answers on what went down with Bruce."

"Bruce, as in Mel's father, Bruce?"

This has my little doll's attention and I wonder if I can use this call to my advantage.

"Yeah. That'd be the one. They aren't buying the story that Mel took him down in self-defense and are threatening with murder charges if I don't bring her in."

"Murder charges? Are they on fucking crack? I mean, I know they're desperate to track down the ringleader of their trafficking ring, but what? They have to be smoking something if they think they'll get anything by putting pressure on that girl."

Spencer sighs, and the long pause that ensues has me a little worried. "Yeah, that's where it gets hairy. Hunter was the first person to enter the cave and they want to question him too. My guess is they're going to try to pin it on him."

"Over my dead fucking body."

"I figured you'd say as much. That's why I've been trying to reach you. I need you to control him when we bring in his girl for questioning. Get your lawyers, brothers, security team—whoever you need to in order to keep him in check, because if he has just one misstep with the boys, they'll take him in and I won't be able to track him once he's in federal custody."

Fucking hell. And there's no way my brother wouldn't freak out if they took his girl. He's so damn protective of her.

My head quickly swivels to Hayley, and I know without a doubt that I'd be the same way with her. Even knowing she's the damn mole, which speaks volumes as to my sheer lack of sanity when it comes to anything concerning her.

And just when I think I couldn't obsess over her more, she mouths, "You okay?"

I've basically told her through my conversation with the sheriff that the feds are wanting to talk to Mel, her best friend, and that they want to question her for murder… but her question and concern are directed toward me instead.

Could it be that she feels this strange and irrational pull too?

"Yo, Matthew. You still there?"

"Yeah, I'm still here." I rip my gaze away from the lovely distraction and try to focus on one shit show at a time. "Did they say when they're bringing her in?"

"As soon as we can locate them." Spencer sighs and I can feel his agitation. *Yeah, you and me both.* "You don't happen to know where they're hiding now, do you?"

"You damn well know they aren't hiding, so don't start giving the feds any ideas. Hunter's been known to go off grid since his teenage years, and now he's continuing the tradition with his future bride. Nothing more nothing less."

"Quite the dream team." Spencer snorts. "Either way, do you know where they are?"

"No. I don't. But if I find out, I'll let them know you're looking for them." I glance at the little thief, debating whether or not to feed her more information. *Fuck it.* If it leaks, then it'll only be further proof that she's the mole. "While I have you on the line, any word on Catherine or

Raul? The man killed his own brother, a notorious cartel leader. The very one who'd been heading the trafficking ring they're supposedly hell bent on uncovering. You'd think that they would want that dynamic duo's location instead of wasting their time on my brother and his fiancé."

"You'd think, but they don't operate on logic. So no, we have no new leads on Catherine and Raul. You know I'd tell you if I did." There's a long pause, before he's whispering into the receiver. "Under your nose."

"What?"

"Alright. Talk soon." Spencer rushes out before I can ask him to repeat what he'd said.

Under your nose. I turn to the right and face the beauty before me. *Is he saying that the key to their location is right under my nose?*

It would definitely track with my theory that Hayley is the mole; that she's the link between our family and the pair of psychopaths that keep eluding us.

This puts me back on guard and I definitely can't let her sneak past my defenses. No matter how tempting she becomes.

If what Spencer is insinuating is true, I can't afford a misstep—and that's exactly what'll happen if I let myself play with my prey.

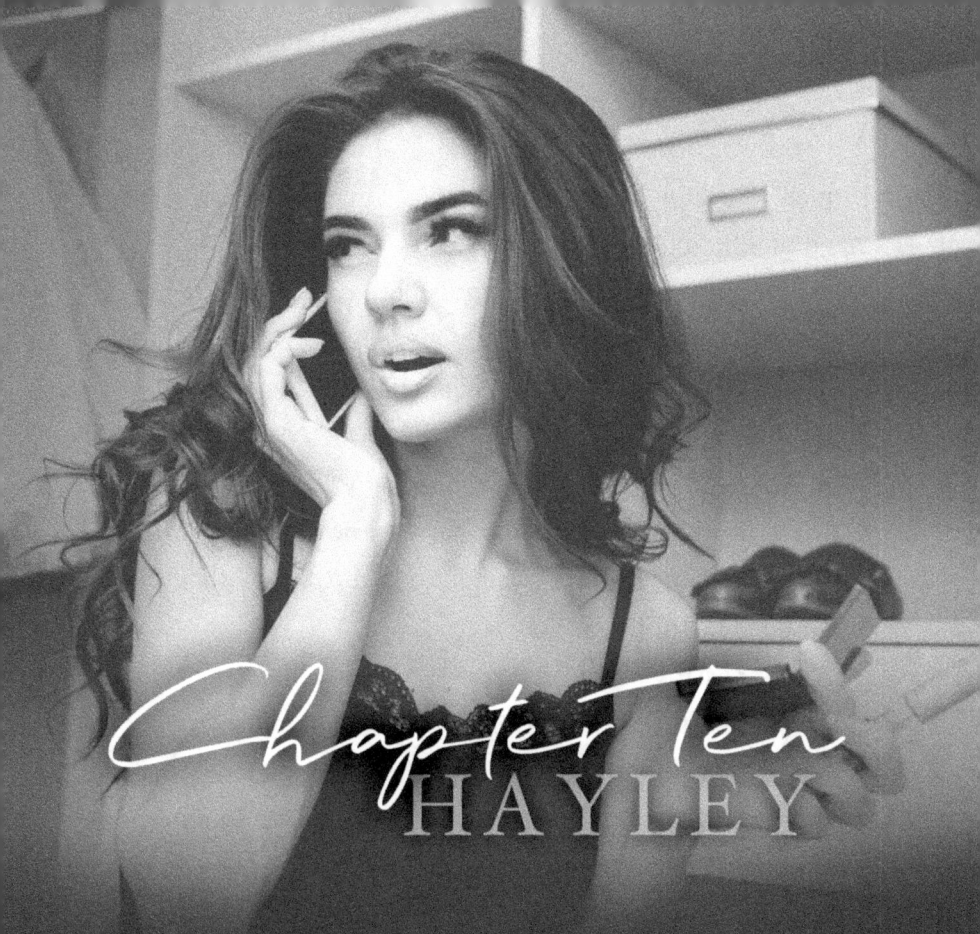

Chapter Ten
HAYLEY

"Oh, Mel! Thank God you're here." I'd been pulling clothes out of my dresser when my friend walks in and I immediately drop what I'm doing to give her a hug.

"Of course!" She hugs me back, her pregnant belly smashing against me before she's placing both of her hands on my shoulders and looking me in the eye. "Hunter and I were heading out of town when he told me about Matt's hare-brained scheme of having you move in with him! I mean, who does that?"

"I know! Can you believe it? I barely even know him and he wants me living with him for three whole months."

My brows furrow and Matthew's talk with the sheriff comes flooding back. "But wait... There's something we need to talk about."

I drag her to the bed, sitting us both on the edge.

"What is it? Did he hurt you? I swear to God, I will end —" Mel gets up, but I pull her hand and bring her back down.

"No, no. This isn't about me. *It's about you.*" I whisper the last three words, needing her to know this is serious. "Look, I'm sure I'm not even supposed to know this, but I can't keep it from you."

This has my friend's brows furrowing deeper and her nose scrunching. "You're freaking me out, Hayley."

"Okay, so I may have overheard a conversation between Matthew and the sheriff. It sounded like he was looking for you, wanting to bring you in and question you... *for murder.*"

I'm expecting my friend to break out into sweats or hysteria, but her face softens instead as her lips break out into a sad smile.

"Oh. That." Her eyes well up, but no tears fall. "Hunter's got that handled. Don't you worry about me."

My jaw drops. "Not worry about you? They want to question you for murder and you're wanting me not to worry? You're my friend. Of course I'm going to worry."

Her smile widens as she pulls me into an embrace. "You're awesome for that, you really are." Mel releases her hold, her eyes glistening with unshed tears. "But trust me, this isn't your monkey, and it's definitely not your circus. We'll get it handled."

She wipes at her eyes, and I see the first tear fall. "But Mel, you're—"

"Stop. Seriously." She holds a palm up and plasters on a cheery smile. "Right now we need to worry about Matthew's kidnapping charges. I'm just thankful Hunter had his SAT phone charged. Otherwise, who knows if we'd been able to track you down. But don't you worry. I have my man talking some sense into that Neanderthal out there."

Her words sink in and the possibility of getting out of this new living arrangement has my stomach a flutter. And not in a good way, which is telling. *Do I secretly want to live with Matthew Crown?*

I've been under the thumb of a man my entire life. Needing to cater to and become the epitome of perfection. You'd think the idea of being under another man's care would repulse me. *Care.* That's where the difference lies. Where my father's care was self-serving, it feels as if with Matthew, he truly has my best interest at heart.

My thoughts flit back to the way he buckled me in to keep me safe, the coffee he gave me—made just the way I like—and then his concern for my driving four hours a day, subjecting me to an increased risk of accidents. *Could all of that be genuine?*

"Earth to Hayley…"

I blink, focusing my eyes only to see Mel's puzzled stare reflected back at me.

"Sorry, got lost in thought there."

"Oh, no. I know that look. And I'm sorry. I should've asked first before sicking Hunter on his brother." Mel rears her head and raises a brow. "Hayley, do you want to stay with Matt?"

I feel my cheeks heat and have to bite my bottom lip to keep myself from grinning.

"Ohhh-mmmm-gggg! Hayley, you sly girl." Melissa is grinning from ear to ear as she rubs her palms together. "Oh, Hunter!"

I leap forward and clap a hand over my friend's mouth, needing to keep her from making the situation worse. "Shh! Don't tell Hunter a damn thing, Mel. Not when I don't even know what's going on inside my head."

Mel nods with my palm still firmly clapped against her mouth, lifting a hand with three fingers and pledging scout's honor.

I drop my hold and giggle. "Girl. You are not a scout. But I'll take it."

"Well, what else was I supposed to do? I couldn't say jack with you going all ninja on me." She rolls her eyes and laughs. "So, care to fill me in on this change of heart? Does this mean you're finally telling your father to fuck off and going after what you really want?"

Now it's my turn to roll my eyes. "I'd say opening my shop is going after what I really want."

"You know what I'm talking about. Matthew. You were smitten with him the night at The Fox and the only reason you denied yourself was because of Parker."

I press my lips together and give her a tight nod. She's right. Of course she is. But I'm not ready to admit it.

"I might've wanted him then, but I know that any way I look at it, it's impossible now. If I let myself have him, then my father will just use it for his own gains. There's no doubt about it. He'll hold it over his head." I pick up the nightgowns I'd dropped on the floor and harshly shove them into a duffel bag. "Besides, all of this is assuming Matthew even wants something with me. Personally, I think he still harbors resentment over our first encounter."

Mel chortles. "Girl, you're delusional if you think that man would *ever* turn you down. Are you forgetting I've been in the same room as you two? The way he looks at you, I swear he'd eat you whole if you'd let him."

My entire body flushes at the thought of that masculine specimen perched between my legs, his lips hovering over my core, ready to kiss and lick it away.

"And there it is." Mel's laughter breaks me out of my fantasy, only for my cheeks to heat further at the realization that I've been caught. "Yeah, just you wait until you've had a taste of the real thing, not just the fantasies in your head."

My friend swoons, placing the back of her hand to her forehead and letting herself fall back onto the bed.

"You act as if it were magic; this life altering thing." I

shake my head and walk toward the closet, pulling out several dresses.

"It is. No, seriously. I know you haven't had much time with Mila or the other Crown women, but we all can say the same." She sits up, her face going solemn. "It's as if your entire life you'd been operating, thinking you were whole, but then these men come into your life and you realize how wrong you'd been. They are the other piece of you. The one you didn't even know you'd need. But now that you've had it, you can't picture your life without it."

I let out a low whistle. "Sounds intense. And I don't want any part of it. Lord knows my father provides enough of that already."

My back is to the room, but that doesn't stop my friend from lopping a pillow at my head.

"You little turd. It's a different kind of intensity. You just wait." I turn to face her and see the smug smile on her face. "Once you've had your taste of a Crown brother, there's no going back."

I snort. "It sounds like a drug—*or worse*. A cult."

This earns me another pillow to the head. "Uh-huh. And you'll be drinking the kool-aid in no time."

"Nope. That isn't happening." I go back to pulling out dresses from my closet with certainty. It's not happening because I can't let it. *I won't let it.* Especially if what she's saying is true.

No, what I need is desensitization therapy. They say cohabitation lets you see someone's true colors, so maybe this is a good thing. I'll see all his flaws and fall out of this weird crush I have on him, all while keeping him at arm's length and doing my job.

It'll be perfect. *Win-win.* He gets the benefit of my marketing genius, and I get over the man that haunts my dreams. I mean, *what could possibly go wrong?*

Matthew

"We've already had this conversation, so just go ahead and pretend like I'm threatening to castrate your balls if you step out of line with Hayley again." Hunter rubs a palm over his face and groans. "But I know it's pointless. You've found your girl and there isn't a man on this earth who could derail this."

He's now waving one hand in my direction and the other toward the bedroom the girls are in.

Funny thing is, *he's right*. Well, as far as feelings go.

But even though there's no stopping how I feel about Hayley, I'm still in control of my actions. And there's no way in hell I can let myself act on what I feel if what Spencer was insinuating is true.

"What I do or don't do with Hayley is none of your damn business. What *is* your business is the sheriff wanting to bring in Mel for questioning."

Hunter's face turns beet red and the rage in his eyes is something I'd only wish on my worst enemy.

"They aren't bringing her in for shit. I'll go instead." He's pacing now and this reaction is exactly what I'd predicted. "No, they'd have to kill me before taking my pregnant bride."

"Brother, that's what they want. Spence said they're looking to pin the sex trafficking ring on someone, and that someone is looking like you." I walk toward him, placing a firm hand on his shoulder and stop his movement. "Look at me. Look at me, Hunter."

He finally lifts his gaze to meet mine, so I continue. "Under no circumstances can you give them what they want. If not for you, then for Mel. Think of her all alone while you rot in some federal prison for a crime you and I both damn well know you didn't commit."

He closes his eyes as his face scrunches together in agony at the very thought. "It's just horse shit, brother. They have two of the ringleaders on the loose. Raul was *El Jefe's* brother, his right-hand man and the one orchestrating all of the moving pieces here in the states. Why aren't they going after him or Catherine at the very least? She knew about it all along. Seems like she's an accomplice to me."

"I know. It makes no sense." I'm rubbing at my temples, trying to understand the reasoning behind it all. "Right now, we just need to figure out how we're going to go about this. I say we get with the men of WRATH securities. They have some of the best defense attorneys on retainer. I'm sure they could hook us up with someone on short notice."

"You're probably right. It's necessary to go in with counsel. Might as well be some of the best in the country."

"Glad you're seeing logic, brother." I clap a hand to his back, thankful as fuck that he didn't put up more of a fight. The Crown men don't tend to see reason when it comes to their women.

My stomach knots and visions of Hayley come to mind. *Fuck.* That girl has a hold on me, and I need to shake it. There's no way she'll ever be a Crown. She's one of *them* —trying to take my family down. I just need to figure out how exactly, and have the tables turned.

Catherine and Raul might be out of reach for the feds, but Hayley's right here.

The answer is simple. Find out how she's tied to the trafficking ring, produce the evidence, and pin the whole thing on her, leaving my brother and his girl in the clear.

Bile crawls up my throat at the very image of Hayley behind bars, but everyone must pay for their sins. *Especially those against a Crown.*

Chapter Eleven
HAYLEY

G*osh, it's beautiful here.* I sit back in my plush office chair and look out the massive picturesque window. It overlooks the snowcapped mountains and I couldn't imagine a more perfect sight.

Sighing deeply, I turn back toward my computer and open up the presentation I've been working on. *It's going to be a closer, I just know it.* Now if I could just find Matthew so I could show it to him, but it's like he's vanished into thin air. Which is absurd because I live with the man.

But it's been three days since I moved in and three days

since I've seen him. It's like living with a ghost. By the time I get up, the coffee is ready and the fireplace is still warm from the fire he'd had on just moments before, and if I didn't know any better, I'd think he was afraid of running into me. *But that's crazy.* Matthew Crown doesn't know the meaning of fear. He's the epitome of strength and virulence.

I sigh, swooning as I click open the web browser.

"I'm not disturbing you, am I?" A familiar voice startles me out of my thoughts, and I look up to see the smarmy man I'd met a few weeks back.

"Radley?" My brows push together, wondering what in the world he's doing here.

"That'd be me, little dove." He smiles, but there's nothing sweet about it. "Heard we'd hired someone to do our marketing. But I didn't know it was someone as purty as you. Bet the boss is tickled pink."

He steps closer until his groin is pressed against my desk and I shudder at the memory of our last encounter. I was leaving work and we were the only two people stepping into the elevator. He'd had a meeting with my father, so I thought surely he wouldn't try any funny business knowing who I was, but man was I wrong.

"Did it hurt, baby?" His words leave me wondering if he's directing them toward me. He could be talking to someone via bluetooth, right?

"I'm sorry. Are you talking to me?"

"Of course I am. So did it hurt?"

"Did what hurt?"

"When you fell from heaven. Such a purty girl like you must be an angel sent from above."

My stomach churns and I take as many steps away from the man as the small space allows. Sure, he's handsome, and very good at what he does based on what Father was saying—but he's got sleazebag written all over.

I may not have much dating experience, but I know what a player looks like and he's like an older, more well-versed version. Extremely dangerous to women everywhere.

Needing to set him straight, I make my lack of interest clear. "Sorry to disappoint, but I'm no angel and I don't appreciate your flirtation."

He chuckles, but there's no humor in it. "Playing hard to get, I see."

I straighten before pressing my shoulder's back and lifting my chin. "No. I'm not playing. I'm extremely serious, and if you don't stop being forward, I'll have no other option but to tell my father you're a fuck-boy. And sir, I can assure you he'll never do business with you again."

The smug bastard purses his lips before stepping so close I have to press my entire body against the elevator wall in order to keep us from touching.

"Little girl, you have it all wrong. It's your father who wants my business, and if he's the man I think he is, then he'd sell his soul to get it and you, little dove, would just be a drop in the bucket."

My bottom lip trembles and I feel the sting in my nose. He's right. Heck, I don't even curse. I bet it came out all shaky and wrong.

I was all bravado and this man saw right through it. I'm not tough and my father doesn't give a damn about me.

I'm frozen. Unable to respond as tears pool in my eyes, when by the grace of God, the elevator door opens and my father's secretary steps in.

"Hayley? What are you still doing here? I thought you'd left a while ago." She's looking at me and then at Radley, her eyes narrowing. "Everything okay?"

"Yes, thank you Natalie. I just forgot something in my office." Not wanting to make more of this encounter than what it is, I play it down and press the button to open the doors once more. "Can you help me find it?"

Her brows slightly raise, but she just nods. "Of course, dear."

I know I don't need her help finding some mythical object, and gauging from how quickly she exits the elevator, I feel she gets it too.

Letting out a sigh of relief as soon as the doors shut behind us, I turn to Natalie and smile. "I'm so sorry, but I didn't forget anything. That guy just gave me the creeps and I didn't want to leave you alone with him after I high tailed it out of there."

She gives me a sympathetic smile and places a hand on my shoulder. "I understand, sweetheart. Do you want to tell your father about it?"

I can tell she's just asking out of courtesy because she and I both know my father won't do a damn thing.

"Thank you, Natalie, but I think it'll be okay. I'll just be sure to steer clear of him and think you should do the same."

"Oh, I will, hun. Don't you worry 'bout me." She winks while opening her bag and shows me her Glock.

Damn. *Natalie is packin'.*

"I didn't know you carried," I whisper-hiss as to not draw attention.

"Sure, do. And I suggest you start as well. Such a pretty girl can never be too safe, especially with creepers like that one." She purses her lips as she walks to the second bank of elevators before pressing the call button.

And as I sit here staring at the very creeper she mentioned, I wish now more than ever that I'd taken her advice. He's just standing there, leering. Even something like pepper spray would make me feel a little safer.

Enough, Hayley. You are *tough. You've got this.*

Needing to get him out of my office as soon as possible, I address him head on.

"I'm sorry. Is there something I can help you with?" I

raise a brow, and even though I'm not one hundred percent where I want to be on the confidence scale, I know I'm much tougher today than when we last met.

"Yea—" Radley starts to say but is immediately cut off by what could only be described as a growl.

"*No.*" Matthew appears at the door frame, his chest heaving as if he'd just ran a mile—and dang is he a sight for sore eyes.

The man is absolutely gorgeous, and I swear he gets hotter every day.

"There you are, boss man. I knew I'd find you here." He shoots Matthew his smarmy smile, and I'm not sure I like what he's implying.

"I *wasn't* in here. You were." He raises a disapproving brow before both eyes narrow. "And why exactly is that?"

Radley chuckles. "I told you. I was looking for you."

He glowers, and every step toward us is more menacing than the last. "And did you find me by pressing yourself against that desk?"

This makes Radley take a few steps back and I finally let out a breath I didn't know I'd been holding. And of course the sudden change in energy doesn't go unnoticed by Matthew, whose face turns a deeper shade of red.

"*Speak.*"

For the first time since meeting Radley, I actually feel bad for him. He's lost all bravado and looks like a dejected little boy.

"No, boss. I swear, I was just looking for you. Didn't mean to step on your girl's toes."

Radley's words have me rearing my head, my face scrunching in disbelief. There's no way he could think me Matthew's girlfriend. The man avoids me like the bubonic plague.

Whatever the reason may be, the smarmy man's words have Matthew's face softening as contentment briefly crosses his face. *Interesting.*

"From now on, you aren't to enter Ms. Barclay's office. She is off-limits to you or the other men in the facility. If you have to address her, you come to me first. Understood?"

Radley smirks while giving him a quick nod. "Crystal clear. I told you you'd—"

"*Enough.*" Matthew roars while cutting him off and pointing toward the door. "Head to my office and we'll talk there."

"Sure thing, boss." Radley just chuckles, but does as he says. "I'll leave you two to it."

What it is, I have no clue, and I'd be lying if I said I wasn't curious. Thankfully, I don't have to wait long because as soon as Radley clears the threshold, Matthew is turning to face me, his intense stare making me suck in a sharp breath.

"We're having dinner at my brother's tonight. You can leave your car at the office. I'll be driving us both."

"Um, excuse me? I haven't seen you in three days. You

can't just come in here and demand things of me that are not work related. Besides, I have plans." My brows push together, not wanting to divulge any more than I have to. But he can't just spring stuff on me.

"Plans?" His eyes narrow as he takes one step closer.

"Yes. Plans. Very common on Friday night." At least they should be for someone my age. Unfortunately, what I have in store is far from common. But then again, few carry the family baggage I do.

"Cancel your *plans*." He closes the distance between us before gripping my jaw with his powerful hand. "I've made it clear. You're mine, and there's no way I'm letting you go off unaccompanied. Besides, Mel needs you."

That dirty little... He knows damn well what he's doing mentioning my friend. I'm only *his* when it comes to work related stuff. Not my personal time.

But I haven't been able to talk to Mel since my apartment and the lack of communication is worrisome.

From the day she came into my shop looking like a bruised peach, we've talked every day. I've made sure of it, even when she's off on her trips with Hunter.

I know it irritates him, but hey, he took me on when he decided to finally seal the deal with my friend.

"So, Mel will be there?"

"Yes, she will." Matthew looks toward the rising sun and, even annoyed as I am, I can't help but stare. His chiseled features are so masculine, I wonder if those hard lines track with the rest of his body as well.

I let my eyes drop to his broad chest, imagining what lies beneath when a soft chuckle has my eyes shooting back up. "Like what you see, doll?"

This makes me roll my eyes. *Of course I like what I see, I'm not blind.* Choosing to ignore his statement, I press him about my best friend.

"Do you know if she's been in to see the sheriff? I haven't been able to get a hold of her and I'm worried."

Matthew's brows push together and he flashes me a look I can't quite place. "No, not yet. We're all going in tomorrow."

I blink back in surprise. "Oh, okay. Let me clear my calendar. I had a call—" I haven't even finished responding when he's turning and heading toward the door.

"You aren't going. It's only the Crown men and their women." His words sting. I know they shouldn't. I'm not part of their family. But I can't help it as my thoughts drift back to that picture on his bar and how happy they all looked. *What would it be like to finally belong?*

I'm not given much time to wallow because Matthew barks out his orders as he vanishes into the hall. "Be ready by six."

"*Asshole.*" I mutter under my breath, only for it to be met with a chuckle.

"I heard that." His trailing voice utters, "Six o'clock, Hayley. Be ready."

This freaking little shit. I curse him out in my head.

Surely he isn't telepathic. And even if he weren't, for once in my life, I don't think I'd mind.

Cursing is sort of cathartic.

Fuck. Fuuuuuuck. Fuuuuuuuuuuuuck.

I sigh deeply, feeling a satisfaction I've never felt before.

"*Fuck. Yes*," I whisper out loud, loving the sound.

Yeah, I think I very much like to curse.

Chapter Twelve
MATTHEW

"Cut the shit and tell me what you were doing in her office." I slam the door behind me and glower at Radley behind the bar, watching him pour whiskey into a glass. "It's a little early for a drink, isn't it?"

He grins, the smile spreading from ear to ear. "Not when we have some celebrating to do!"

The fucker looks positively radiant as he walks toward me, two tumblers in hand.

"And what exactly are we celebrating?" I raise a skeptic brow and take the proffered shot.

"Two things. First, I closed that NYC deal. You're now

the premium brand of choice for all the Hastings Hotels." This has my brows shooting up. I thought for sure he was going to get turned down by the pompous heiress. But then again. He has a way with the ladies. "And second, I knew that girl would be perfect for you. Seems like I was right."

My raised brows drop almost instantly. "Look, I don't know what you've concocted in that head of yours, but there's nothing going on between Hayley and me. You damn well know her father's been after our company and I thought I'd get some free labor while I mull over his offer. *That's it.* That's all there is."

Radley raises a brow, a smirk playing on his lips before he's shooting back the celebratory whiskey. "You say that, boss, but it looked to me like you ran clear across the property just to make it to her office in time. You wouldn't be doing that unless you had a stake in that girl. Care to dispute that?"

This little fucker. He isn't wrong. Question is, how'd he know it?

I throw back the drink and slam down the tumbler onto the desk. "And what makes you say that?"

"You were sweatin' like a whore in church, your chest heaving like you'd just ran a four-minute mile. Building's air conditioned and there's no way you were down in the gym dressed like that." He waves a hand up and down at me. "Leaves only one answer. You ran in from outside and I know I didn't see you by the entrance when I got here."

He's pursing his lips, like he's pinned the tail on the donkey.

And he has. Yes, I've been avoiding running into Hayley, trying to avoid a repeat of what happened in the truck. I can't help it. When I'm around that girl, all rational thought leaves my head and all I want to do is pin her to the floor and rut her like an animal.

Even now, my cock is still at half-mast from having been near her. So, yes. I've been avoiding her. But that doesn't mean I haven't been keeping an eye on the little thief.

I have to catch her breaking her facade, and I can't do that if I'm not around. *My solution?* Cameras. They're everywhere. Including her office. And as soon as I was alerted to Radley's presence, you bet your ass I ran clear across the fucking property.

There's no way in hell I'm letting him near her. I have no doubt he just seduced the infamous hotel heiress—a finicky woman—and that's how he closed this deal. What could he do with Hayley in just a matter of minutes? I don't know, and I sure as fuck am not willing to find out.

Am I jealous? Nah. I just don't want him messing with my plan. That's all.

"So, want to take me out for steak? Celebrate this massive account I just landed you?"

Radley's words shake me back into the present. "Can't tonight. Dinner with the family, but tell you what." I hand him the contents of my new wallet. "Whatever debauchery you have in store tonight, it's on me."

He counts the numerous hundred-dollar bills, running his tongue along the ridge of his teeth as he walks toward the door. "Thanks, boss. It's gonna be one hell of a night."

"Just keep the details to yourself. I don't want to hear about you catching some other VD." I shudder as he exits, softly shutting the door behind him.

Some men think it's a flex to pull a new girl every night, but that couldn't be further from the truth. The more time passes, I've come to realize that my brothers are really on to something.

The real flex is finding one woman to share your life with. One who'll have your back no matter what. Like Mel with Hunter. She full-well knows they're going to pin Bruce's death on him and she isn't willing to let him go down for her. She's adamant that he stays back while they question her, but the foolish girl must not get it yet.

When a Crown man has found his match, he'd rather burn in hell than watch his precious love suffer for even one damn second.

Hayley's frown flashes in my mind's eye and my stomach churns. I may not want to admit it to myself, but my subconscious is sure trying hard to make me see.

If I were being honest with myself, the thought of that girl's discomfort makes me absolutely homicidal.

I'm fucked. That's all there is to it.

So what if I like her? So what if she ends up being my

match? *I can't have her.* She's off limits and nothing I can say or do will change that. No matter what, I will never bed with someone who's out to hurt my family.

I'm loyal, and that's a line I'll *never* cross.

Hayley

"They've been in there for hours." The brunette named Pen sighs while rocking a baby in her arms. Her child is absolutely gorgeous, and it's no surprise because he takes after both her mother and father, Jack. *Another Crown man that's built like a Greek god.*

"You know how they are when there's something going down." Anaya, a blonde woman with piercing blue eyes, retorts while flipping channels on the massive screen. She's married to Austin, and although he looks different from the rest of the brothers, he's still drool worthy in his own right.

Not that I was drooling... *okay, maybe just a little.*

"Yeah. It just feels like there's always something going down. We need a break from the drama." Mel whines as she plops down next to me in the massive u-shaped sectional.

We're in the game room at the Crown Ranch, and all the women are gathered around while the brothers take a call with their security team. Yes. Apparently, this family needs its own security team.

To be honest, it's all been a little overwhelming,

meeting everyone, keeping their names straight and piecemealing their history together.

At least I already know Mila and Mel from high school. They're tied to Jace and Hunter, and it's a good thing everyone's so dang nice. Even the kids were sweet.

And this place. *Wow.* It's absolutely gorgeous. The main building is a grand farmhouse, painted in white with a wraparound porch built for sippin' tea and watching the sun set.

The property hosts multiple cabins where people come to vacation, and from what the girls have said, their guest list is pretty impressive.

"You're so right, Mel. But at least we aren't in lockdown this time." Mila purses her lips before taking a sip of her post dinner coffee.

We had the most amazing roast with mashed potatoes, topped off with a five-layer chocolate cake—*Anaya's mother's specialty*. It's sinfully decadent, and even though I'm still full from dinner, who can turn down coffee and cake? *Not me.*

"Lockdown?" I mumble as I take another swipe at the chocolate ganache, moaning at the explosion of flavor dancing across my tongue.

"I know, right? Mary's cake really *is* the best." Penelope smiles while getting up before walking over to a frilly bassinet. "And yes, lockdown. First one happened before I was kidnapped."

"Second happened before mine and Pen's impromptu

trip to Mexico." Anaya speaks up, rubbing at her pregnant belly and raising her brows. "That's a trip I definitely won't be forgetting."

"Hey, let's not forget the time Mel and I went missing." Mila, who's also heavily pregnant, waves a hand in the air before pointing a finger at me. "Come to think of it, you're probably next."

Everyone breaks out into laughter except for me. I don't think this is funny. *At all.*

"Um...excuse me, but it seems like being a Crown woman should come with a warning." I'm still not laughing and they're totally snickering now.

"Well, Hayley, consider this your official warning." Anaya smirks, and her words have me choking on a piece of cake.

Coughing, I manage to eek out, "What?"

"Girl, don't act all surprised. That man is smitten with you." Penelope purses her lips while rocking the bassinet with one hand.

"Sure is." Mila grins. "I have *never* seen that man look at a woman the way he does you, and I'd say it's only a matter of time before you two are getting hitched."

"Ha! Fat chance of that ever happening. I think you must be confusing the look of derision with whatever it is you think you're seeing. Matthew Crown can barely stand to be around me. Even goes out of his way to avoid me." I think back to the lonely mornings in his apartment and know these women are wrong.

Mel shakes her head, and I realize she's been awfully quiet until this point. "You're living in his home, Hayley. That, in and of itself, speaks volumes."

"Yeah. *That he's a masochist.* I'm telling you; we end up fighting or arguing whenever we're alone together." I roll my eyes while taking a sip of coffee, attempting to wash down their words right alongside my delicious cake.

"You keep telling yourself that, babe. Meanwhile, we know what's up. I'm betting on a fall wedding." Mel rubs her hands together while waggling her brows. "Any takers?"

"Ha! Sara would keel over!" I giggle, picturing that viper with plumes of smoke coming out of her ears.

"Sara? The one who works at the distillery?" Mel's brows furrow and I realize I hadn't filled her in on the drama.

"That'd be the one. She's such a bitch." I spit out the words before I can fully think them through, and this earns me a gasp from both Mila and Mel.

"Who is this and what has she done with my sweet little friend?!" Mel shoves at my shoulder, demanding an answer, and I can't help but laugh.

"It's Hayley 2.0, and she's sort of a *bad bitch*." I smirk while the entire room erupts in a mixture of cheers and laughter.

"It's about damn time!" Mel beams, her smile stretching from ear to ear. "Now, how about taking that attitude and sharing it with your father? Just make sure you give me front row seats to that show. I've been waiting for it for quite some time."

"Ha! *You've* been waiting? It's practically been my life mission, overcoming that bull shit trauma."

My friend just grins at me while Mila pipes in. "Look at you, cursing up a storm now. I gotta say, I'm loving the new 'no fucks given' version of you."

I sigh, letting her words sink in. "Yeah, you and me both, girl. But speaking of fathers, what's going on with the whole Bruce situation? I haven't been able to reach you for the past three days and I've tried asking Matthew about it, but like I said before, he can't run out of the room fast enough whenever we're together."

Silence. I'm greeted with nothing but silence. Even the baby isn't making a peep, and I bet if the other kids weren't in bed already, they'd be quiet too.

"Okay. Anyone care to fill me in on what's going on?" I speak up after even more reticence, only for it to be met with awkward glances between the women. "Someone? Anyone? Hell, I'll even take answers from the baby."

This earns me a soft smile from Mel, who finally answers. "We're going into the sheriff's office in the morning. Hunter didn't want me to go, but I told him there was no way on God's green earth that I'd stay back and watch him basically incriminate himself for me."

My mouth is hanging open as I stare at my friend in disbelief. "So, they're really going to question you for murder?"

Mel slowly nods. "The thing is, I did kill Bruce, but in self-defense. He'd captured my mother and kept her chained to a wall for years. Right along with the other women he'd been trafficking."

If I thought my mouth had been hanging open before, it's now totally unhinged. "Mel—"

"I know. It's this huge, convoluted mess." She pulls my hand into her lap in an attempt to comfort me when it should totally be the other way around.

"Convoluted mess? That's the understatement of the century. This is…" My hands are flailing in the air, trying to find a word that's adequate enough to describe how terrible this all is. "Horrific and traumatizing, to say the least!"

"And you don't even know the half of it. Turns out Bruce had been smuggling trafficked women for this cartel, and somehow the feds think that by bringing me in they'll get to my father's accomplices."

"But that doesn't make any sense." My brows push together as I try to find logic in her words.

"I know. They must think that I have information on my father's connections—whoever he worked with in order to get the women across state lines. But I can't give them names I don't have. I'm telling you, Bruce being such a machiavellian degenerate was as much a surprise to me as it was to everyone else."

"*Jesus.* I'm so sorry, Mel."

"It's okay. It'll be okay." My friend pats my hand, but I honestly don't see how there's anything 'okay' about this.

"She's right. Either way, it'll be fine. We always find a way out." Anaya sips on her coffee, her expression solemn as Mila adds, "Yup. That's probably what the men are doing now. Finding a way out of this. I just hope it doesn't involve another lockdown."

This makes me groan. "It doesn't sound like they're very effective anyway."

The women burst into laughter, but I still don't find it funny and based on their less than stellar kidnapping history, I'm definitely not going to leave this up to the men. My friend is in danger of being locked up for life and that's something I'm not taking lightly.

The men can have their meetings and lockdowns, *but I'm sure as hell not standing down.*

Chapter Thirteen
MATTHEW

"What's the plan for tomorrow?" I pull a cigar out of the humidor and cut it before making my way to the leather chesterfield.

"Same one we'd discussed before, brother." Austin sits down in one of the wingback chairs with his back to the roaring fire. We're in Jack's office, a room that's held many tough conversations and much needed revelations—and I suspect today will be no different.

"Well, I don't agree with that plan and apparently neither does your girl. Our women might act all meek and docile, but they're just as ferocious about protecting their men as we are to them." I light the cigar and take a puff, realizing that the entire room has gone deathly silent.

I see all eyes are on me, but it's Hunter who breaks first. "So when was it? And you fuckers better pay up because I know I've won this one."

My brows push together. "What the fuck are you talking about? When was what?"

"You said our women are just as ferocious about protecting us as we are to them. That, my brother, would imply that you've already claimed Hayley as your own." Hunter lifts his rocks glass in my direction as he takes the opposite chair from Austin. "Go on then. Spit it out. We've all been taking bets on how long it would take you to pull your ass out of your head, and I think I'm about to be the victor."

I scoff. "You're delusional. I misspoke. That's it." Hunter raises a skeptic brow and I turn to my other brothers, seeing a similar look on their faces. "I'm serious. She's the fucking mole. I would never betray our family like that."

"Okay. Let's say she's the mole then." Jack sits behind his desk and picks up his phone. "Let's call the sheriff and tell him as much. I'm sure he'll be able to feed her to the feds and—"

I'm standing before he's even finished his sentence, ripping the receiver out of his hands and chucking the entire thing across the room in one swift move.

Fuck. This asshole just played me and as his lip tilts up in a smirk, I know I've shown my hand.

They know it. I know it. *I'm fucked.*

Hunter appears behind me, clapping a hand on my back. "Good thing she isn't the mole, brother. The sooner you accept that, the happier you both will be."

I stumble backward, running both hands through my hair. "*Jesus.* She just can't be the mole."

"She isn't." Spencer steps into the office, drawing everyone's attention.

"How'd you get in?" Jack's eyes narrow as he looks at one of Hunter's longtime friends.

"Mary let me in. Even said she'd pack some of that chocolate cake of hers."

"Yeah." Jack chuckles, but it's dry. "That just means there's less cake for me."

"Hey, what's this about my Hayley not being the mole?" *My Hayley.* Okay. I'm just going with it now, and it seems my brothers are too, because none of them even bat an eye.

"She isn't. Her father has his own can of worms—tax evasion, money laundering. The list goes on and on. But she's free and clear of anything relating to the trafficking ring."

Spencer's words have a lead ball forming in my gut. *Lord. How fucked is her father?* I'm now glad, more than ever, to have sold no part of Tortured Crown. She may not be the mole I initially thought, but it's clear she'd been working for that snake. Maybe there's a link between the dirt Spencer holds and Hayley's actions.

"Hey, is there any way you can send me what you have on him? I want to make sure it's legit before declining Barclay's offer to buy any of my shares."

Spencer nods. "Sure thing. I'll print them out when you're all down at the office tomorrow. And speaking of, that's why I'm here. I need to know what to expect. With the feds in town, I can't afford a misstep. My department's already under investigation with all the crazy shit we've had happen here in the last two years."

Jack is the first to answer. "Mel is going in with reinforcements. She'll be accompanied by the men of WRATH, as well as two of their top attorneys."

"And you bet your ass I'll be there too." Hunter quips, as if any of us had a doubt.

"I get why you're going," Spencer stops mid-sentence before eyeing us all down. "Just make sure y'all keep him in check. I don't have to remind you what'll happen if he falls into federal custody."

"No, you sure don't." I roll my eyes and sigh. "What you can do is explain to me why you said that the answer to Catherine and Raul's location was right under my nose. The sooner we find the pair, the sooner they stop looking to pin this on my family."

"I meant Mel or her brother Ericson. Even though they might not have outright information on their father's connections, they may've been privy to names or faces of people who came in and out of their home."

This has Hunter snorting. "You know damn well my girl stopped living with that man as soon as I found her trying to jump off that cliff."

"Right. But she was fifteen. It's possible she could identify someone, anyone, who could lead us to Catherine and Raul." Spencer rubs at his scruff as his eyes narrow. "And her brother, well, he definitely spent more time with his old man. Maybe he should come into the station as well."

"Whoa, there. That's a fucking stretch." Austin chimes in while glaring at Hunter. "Just because you see family all the time, it doesn't mean that you're privy to their dirty fuckin' lies."

Jesus. He's still pissed at him for holding back the truth on his bio-dad. I get it. I really do. But his hands aren't the cleanest either. For fuck's sake, he'd been researching the cartel behind our backs—even took that trip down to Mexico that ended up getting his first wife killed! Granted, she was a lying, cheating bitch. *But still.*

"Why do I get the feeling this has nothing to do with Bruce and his offspring?" Spencer looks between Austin and me, catching on to the underlying tension.

"Because it doesn't." Jack sighs. "Look, if you want to bring in Ericson, that'll have to happen when the big boys aren't there. I'm not adding additional fuel to the fire. If they want him, they'll need a fucking subpoena."

Spencer's eyes narrow. "Even if it means getting Mel out of the crossfire?"

This has Hunter's brows shooting up, but Jack speaks before he can get his two cents in. "He's family. Like it or not, and we don't throw family under the bus."

I can see Hunter's internal battle. It's written all over his face.

It's clear that he'd gladly throw Ericson under the bus, roll over him and back up to hit him again, if that's what it took to save his girl. Sad part is, I don't blame him one bit.

I mean, he isn't *really* family, is he?

"If that's your stance, then fine." Spencer shakes his head in obvious disapproval. "Just let me know if anything changes. As it stands, Mel is coming in and Hunter will stay outside of the questioning room while she's at the station. Agreed?"

"Agreed." All but one repeat.

"*Hunter?*" Jack prompts my twin, who's looking anything but sure. "We've talked about this before. Mel will be safe if she follows her counsel's lead."

"Yeah, but you and I both know just how crooked they can be." He turns toward Spencer before adding, "No offense."

"None taken." The sheriff dips his head in acknowledgment. "Let's just say they don't have the cleanest reputation. But I'll do everything in my power to keep your girl safe."

Hunter raises a brow. "I'll hold you to it."

"Good. Now that we have that settled, let's go see what the women are up to." Jack stands from behind his desk as Spencer chuckles.

"I'll leave y'all to that. I have a slice of chocolate cake with my name written all over it, and I'm not about to lose it."

I snort at that. Mary's cake really *is* that good. I swear, that woman could make a leather shoe taste amazing. Give her flour and sugar, and no man or woman stands a chance.

Just then Jace rushes past the sheriff, "Yeah, well, you're gonna have to fight me for that slice!"

"*Motherfucker*," Spencer mutters before turning to sprint through the threshold.

"Children. The lot of them." Hunter mumbles. "I'd much rather shove my face between Mel's legs than a slice of fucking cake."

I chuckle. "Well, I bet Jace would too if Mila didn't have him in the doghouse right now."

We step into the hallway as Jack's booming laughter sounds off behind us. "That's right! He withheld the fact that Mel was getting questioned until the very last minute. Can't fuck with those two. They're more than besties. What is it they call themselves?"

"Soul sisters." Hunter rolls his eyes. "And now it looks like they've taken Hayley in. Yet another cock-blocker."

We're stepping into the family room when all eyes land on us. Mel's specifically trained on her man. "Excuse me? Who are you calling a cock-blocker?"

Penelope giggles as Jack lifts her into his arms, wrapping her legs around his waist. "How about we let the squabbling hens watch the little prince while you and Daddy go fuck?"

A squeak has my eyes darting left only to be met with Hayley's face and penetrating stare. Her focus is on Jack and Pen, and it's clear that she's enraptured.

"Oh, for fuck's sake," Austin groans as he pulls Anaya to her feet, bringing her in for a hug. "I don't know how many times I have to tell you. I don't care to see this bullshit."

His outburst makes me chuckle. I mean, I don't blame him. Pen was his stepdaughter, and she ended up marrying his brother. Even though they aren't blood, it doesn't take a rocket scientist to see how disturbed he was at finding these two out.

"Excuse me, I'm still waiting for an answer on who's the cock-block." Mel purses her lips as Hunter sits beside her before swiftly pulling her onto his lap.

"Are you denying the fact that you can't kiss me in front of your friends?" My brother raises a brow while gripping Mel's jaw, bringing it a hair's breadth away from his lips.

Looking over at Hayley, I see her lips part as her eyes dart back and forth between all the couples. Yes, they're all very affectionate, and no they aren't apologetic about it. *Why should they be?*

Leaving the others in their own little worlds, I walk toward my girl and extend a hand.

"Matthew?" Her nose scrunches in that adorable way and it takes everything in me not to pluck her from the couch.

With as much restraint as possible, I softly utter my command.

"Come. It's time for bed." Hayley's face flushes a deeper shade of red and I realize what I've just implied. Needing to rectify it, I speak again. "Sleep, baby. It's time for sleep."

She blinks a few times before a warm smile spreads across her full lips and she's placing her hand in mine.

Home. That's what her touch feels like. This deep sense of comfort and belonging. Like she's always been mine.

And as we leave the other love birds behind, I can't help but think—*mole or not*—that I've truly found my match.

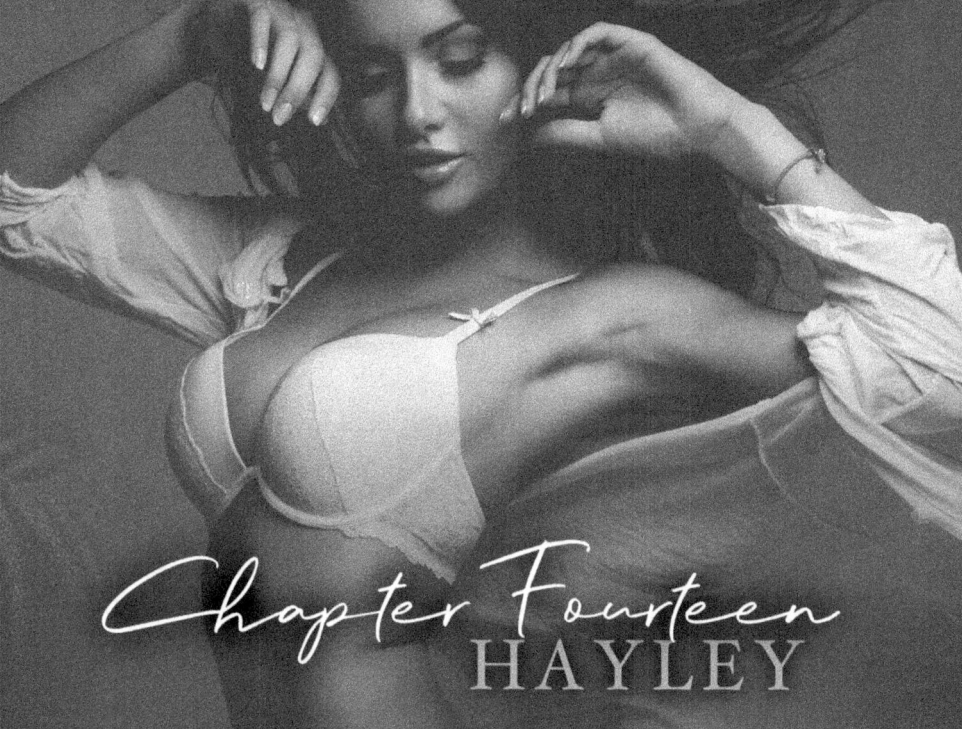

Chapter Fourteen
HAYLEY

We're halfway through the hallway when Matthew's words finally sink in. *Bed? Sleep? What the fuck?*

To be honest, I was under a contact-high from all the lust around us and I wasn't thinking clearly. All it took for me to follow was the look in his eyes and the promise of a bed.

This is crazy. I plant my feet and come to a stop, causing Matthew to take a step back or risk pulling my arm out of its socket.

"Hayley?" He looks confused, as if I should know

what's going on and this is all completely normal.

"Yeah, uh... where are we going?"

"To bed." His brows furrow deeper before he's shaking his head. "I mean sleep. We have to be at the station first thing in the morning. It doesn't make sense for us to drive two hours south, only to turn around and drive back at five in the morning."

"*Okay.* That makes sense, but I didn't think you wanted me coming to the station. Besides, I didn't bring any of my things. I don't even have my toothbrush!"

"I know. But there's been a change of plans." He sighs while rubbing a palm over his face. "Mel is going to need all the support she can get, and let's just say... I've learned from my brother's mistakes. I will not be the man that separates all of you. And as for your things, that's why we're going back to your condo."

This has my jaw dropping. "Excuse me? What?"

"Your place is twenty-minutes over the ridge. It beats the two-hour drive, and it holds most of your belongings."

I don't have time to process his logic because he's taking my hand in his and walking us toward the front door before I've even answered.

Do I want this? Do I want Matthew Crown spending the night in my home?

As I trail behind him, my eyes drifting from where our hands connect to the chisel of his jaw, I know the answer. *Yes.* Yes, I very much do.

I'd be lying if I said otherwise.

Despite his overbearing and demanding ways, I can't help but feel safe whenever I'm with him. It's as if he fills this void I've held onto for so long. And every time he touches me, every time we connect, those dark parts of my heart light up and feel warmth.

For someone who's lived her life in the shadows, begging for scraps of love, this feels like I've won the jackpot.

"Picking you up, doll." His hand drops from mine, only to go toward my waist, where he grips me tight before hoisting me into his truck.

I secretly love when he does this. It makes me feel so small and protected. Coveted as he reaches across me and buckles me in.

Right on cue, I shiver. *He cares*. He truly cares about my safety.

"You okay, sweetheart?" Matthew's hazel eyes search mine, but I don't answer. I can't. Not when I don't know it myself.

It sort of feels like I'm free-falling into this man, loving everything about him, including his surly disposition and domineering ways.

Seconds pass without my answer and concern riddles Matthew's face. "Baby," He goes to pull back, but his arm accidentally brushes against my nipples, and I can't hold back the soft moan.

Instantly, Matthew's eyes darken, the inky black swallowing any trace of gold they once held. "Baby," he repeats, only this time it's five octaves deeper.

"Yes, Daddy?" I whimper.

"*Christ.*" Matthew throws his head back and growls. "Keep talking to me like that, doll, and I'll have no choice but to fuck you right here in the open."

Oh my god. His words have my thighs clenching and a warm tingling sensation spreading right from my core up to my tummy.

"That's what you want, don't you? My girl needs her Daddy right the fuck now." With deft hands, he undoes my seatbelt, the palm of his hand gripping my ribcage before slowly trailing up until he's cupping a breast.

Oh fuck. Oh fuck. Oh fuuuuuck.

I'm panting now, unable to hide my reaction to his touch. It's like crack and I'm his little fiend.

And if I thought I was overheating before, I'm downright melting when his fat thumb strokes my swollen nipple. Once. Twice. It has me squirming, needing something more. What that is, I have no clue. All I know is that if I don't get it, I'm sure to combust.

"*Please,*" I beg for relief. I need it.

Thankfully, he complies.

"I've got you, baby." And he sure does.

Picking me up as if I were nothing more than a rag doll, Matthew carries me toward the bed of his truck, lowering the tailgate and laying me down slow. I'm facing the stars, and they've never shined brighter.

"Listen here, doll. This'll be quick because what I have planned for that little pussy is going to need a hell of a lot more time than we've got." He's lifting the skirt of my dress inch by inch, ever so slowly, dragging his calloused fingertips along my thighs on his way up to my hips. "But don't you worry that pretty little head. You're gonna feel real good."

And with those words, his fingers dig into my hips, dragging me down toward the edge of the bed and pressing my core right to the hard bulge in his pants.

"*Oh, God,*" I moan before whispering, "*So good.*"

The pressure on my engorged clit is too delicious. I need more.

Like a wanton woman, I can't help but shamelessly grind on the thick ridge. Back and forth, I pivot my hips and watch as this man's face transforms right before me.

His intense focus dissolves and nothing but heat burns behind his eyes. "Behave, doll. Or I'll pop that cherry on the bed of this truck, and we both know you deserve better."

Matthew's hand goes to my silk panties, ripping them off with one swift pull. *Damn, that was hot.*

"Beautiful. Just like I knew she would be." He's looking down at my core in reverie. "She's smooth and slick, ready to take this fat cock."

My lips part as a mixture of shock and desire comes over me at the crudeness of his words. Whatever this is, I love it. It makes me ache and burn, hearing him claim me the way he does.

Without preamble, he pushes my thighs wide open, the cool night air hitting my damp slit and making me shiver. Goosebumps riddle my flesh and I'm not sure if it's the outdoor temperature or the nerves and anticipation—whatever it is, it all goes out the window as soon as his warm tongue delivers its first tantalizingly slow lick up my slit.

Holy shit. I was right. It's a cult, and I'm its latest devotee.

M<small>ATTHEW</small>

Mine. That's what she tastes like.

I take another slow swipe of heaven on earth and wonder why in the fuck I'd been holding back all of this time. Her sweet little cunt could've been mine all along, and instead I'd been letting something stupid like my wallet being stolen get in the way.

Fuck it. This girl could steal my damn soul, and I'd give it freely. I belong to her. Every bit of me.

I roll the tip of my tongue over her swollen clit and the gasp it elicits is absolute perfection. My girl arches her back, allowing my palms to move up from around her ass cheeks up to her tiny waist.

She's fucking delicious. I lift my gaze to hers and see

those perky tits thrusted into the air, and damn, I'm dying to see what they look like bare.

My girl whimpers as I pull my mouth from her sweetness, but it's nothing compared to the little yelp she gives me as I take the collar of her dress and rip it clear down the center.

"*Jesus.* You really are God's gift to mankind." But the thought of others coveting what's mine makes my blood boil and I can't hold back the growl it elicits. "Too bad. I don't plan on sharing."

"What?" Hayley looks dazed as I cup both of her full breasts in my large hands, kneading them before giving them both a quick little slap and watching them bounce before me. God damn, they're perfect. Needing a taste, I lower my mouth and wrap my lips around a fat nipple, rolling the hard little nub with my tongue before biting down on it and pulling.

"*Oh, fuck...* Matthew." Hayley whines as her long slender legs wrap around me, her hot little pussy pressing hard against my stomach. "More. I need more."

I take her deeper into my mouth and give her full tit one more pull before I'm dropping wet kisses all the way down to her core. *It's intoxicating.* The scent of brown sugar and honey makes me hungry for every inch of her delectable body, and I can't wait until I have more time to explore.

Teasing her further, I run the hard tip of my nose along her drenched slit before circling the little pearl that sits atop, pausing to take in the scent that's all her. *Mine.* I growl into her heat, claiming it before devouring it whole.

And like a man starved, I finally put my baby out of her misery and thrust my tongue deep into her channel.

Hayley bucks those wide hips, but Daddy isn't having it. She's going to take this pleasure, over and over, until she's realized there's no life without it. And as her hands dig deep into my scalp, and she utters the words I'd been longing to hear, I know I'm on the right track.

"Yes. Yours." Hayley grinds herself on my face, pressing her sweet little cunt hard against my lips. She's full-out panting now. Her breath coming out in sharp little bursts. "Daddy. Yes. Yours. All. Yours."

Fuckin' straight you are. There's nothing more I want than to shove myself into that tight channel and make it official. Claiming her virgin pussy as my own. Being the only man that will ever have the pleasure and honor of knowing such bliss.

But I can't. Not now. She deserves better.

For now, this'll have to do. I release one of my hands from its death grip on her hip and hover my thumb over the button to her release.

I thrust my tongue in sync with every swirl of my thumb and it's not long before my baby is unravelling for her daddy, her back arching and head lolling back as a string of incoherent babble comes out of her pretty mouth.

"*Ohmyfuckinggod, whatthefuckholyshit… yes, yes,*

yessssss." There she is. My sweet little doll turned hot little whore. *She truly is perfection.*

Chapter Fifteen
HAYLEY

I'm still floating on cloud nine when we enter my condo. Bliss. This is what it must feel like.

"Let's get to bed. We have an early morning." Matthew's gruff voice commands from behind and I can't stop the shiver it elicits.

"Yes, sir." I playfully raise a brow and purse my lips. "The bedroom is this way."

"Oh no, little doll. I'm taking the couch." He shakes his head while raising a palm. "There's no chance in hell I'm keeping my hands off you if I step a foot in that room.

Sleeping next to you all night long? Yeah, that's a surefire way to end up with my cock shoved deep inside you."

The crassness of his words has my pussy clenching and mouth parting open. *I want that. I really want that.* But I can't have it, and at least it looks like he's come to his senses too.

"You're right. What we did out in your truck, that was way out of line, and it can't happen again. My father sent me to work *for* you, not *under* you. It isn't appropriate."

This has Matthew pausing right in front of the hallway that splits off the living area and the bedrooms, his brow lifting in a high arch.

"Little girl, if you think this," he points a finger back and forth between us, "isn't happening, then you're sorely mistaken. You're mine now and I'm yours. There's no going back, and if I have to take you into that room and claim what's mine just to prove it, then fuck it—I'm doing it. Early morning be dammed."

He takes the two steps toward me and hoists me over his shoulder, swatting my ass and making me squeak as he turns and walks down the hall.

I'm hanging upside down with my face to his lower back, and God, what a beautiful sight. *Delicious.* His firm ass has my eyes hooding and mouth drooling.

Snap out of it, Hayley!

"Wait, Matthew!" I can't let this happen. I can't let it go any further without coming clean. "There's something I have to tell you."

He lowers me onto the bed as if I were the most delicate flower. "Shh, I know, baby. And it's okay. You could steal my goddamn soul and I'd give it to you freely."

I feel my nose crinkle and brows scrunch together. Although his words are beautiful, I have no idea what he's talking about. What does his soul have to do with my father?

I'm about to ask him what he means when an all too familiar voice comes calling from the hall.

"Hayley, what the fuck are you doing here? I got an alert that your alarm had gone off, and here you are." My father's agitated voice is getting closer, and I'm so thankful that Matthew had the foresight to close the bedroom door behind us. Having my father walk into a compromising situation isn't exactly ideal.

"Father, I'm indecent. Don't come in." My words have Matthew's brows raising, but his presence alone gives me strength to take a stand, even if it's a small one. "And this is my apartment. I should be the one asking *you* that."

Footsteps stop right outside the door, and he's close enough for me to hear his irritated sigh. "I told you, Hayley. You're supposed to be seducing that Crown boy. How in the fuck are you supposed to do that from all the way here? You told me that man wanted you living with him, yet here you are. Another stupid decision on your part."

Shame floods me as he divulges his disgusting plan, all in front of the only man I've ever lusted over. I'm too embarrassed. I can't even look at him right now.

Unfortunately for me, Matthew has other plans. With two fingers under my chin, he lifts my face toward his. He's standing at the edge of the bed. Meanwhile I'm kneeling, sitting back on my hind legs, having to crane my neck to let him see my chagrin.

"Is it true? Were you sent to tempt me, little doll?" He's whispering, his words coming out low and gruff, but there's no denying the pain that lingers behind his eyes. *Betrayal.* It's written as clear as day.

I can't lie to him, so I nod, unable to form the actual words. I'm a horrible human for even letting it get this far. He must think the worst of me, that none of this is real. *But it is, it so is.*

"Matthew, I—" I try to tell him as much, but he seals my lips with his thumb, slowly caressing the seam back and forth before he does the unexpected—*speaking directly to my father.*

"Why was she sent to seduce me, Mr. Barclay?" Matthew's voice is firm, commanding an answer, yet it lacks all emotion, even as he takes that thumb he'd been caressing me with and shoves it hard into my mouth.

Without removing his eyes from mine, he growls, "*Suck.*"

My eyes prickle with tears, but I do as he says, taking him into my mouth and swirling the fat digit around my tongue. I'm watching the anger in his face dissipate just a bit when it hits me. *This.* I'll make him feel better like this.

"Mr. Crown?" Father squeaks.

"No, it's the Queen of Sheba," Matthew growls, sucking in a sharp breath as I nibble on the tip of his finger. "Of course it's me. Or does your daughter entertain various men in her home?"

His brow is raised, obvious skepticism written all over his face, and it hurts. It truly does. Yes, I know I was sent to deceive him, but everything I've shared with him was special. *He's special.*

"What?! Of course not, I've made sure of it. Always keeping tabs on her, making sure she doesn't associate with anyone not worthy of the Barclay name. I can assure you, that girl is pure as the snow is white."

Father's rambling has Matthew's face transforming from skepticism to full-out rage. His eyes narrow and jaw tightens as he swiftly flips me over, my back now on the bed as he drags me head first to the edge.

He doesn't stop until my head is practically hanging off, the angle letting me see his lip curl just as he asks his next question.

"So what? You sent your virgin daughter to me *for what*? What was she supposed to do?" The disgust is written all over his face, but there's more. There's hurt. His eyes glisten as he shoves down his pants and the most beautiful dick I've ever seen springs out.

Granted, my experience is limited to what I've seen online, but his is by far the best. Thick and long, and the tip, it's leaking. A clear little pearl forms at the head and I can't hold back—*so I don't*. I crane my neck and lick.

Instantly, Matthew's legs shake and he lets out a low hiss as his strong hands grip on to either side of my head, his thick digits biting into my scalp.

"Answer me, Mr. Barclay." His fingers squeeze and the hold is almost painfully hard. "What was your daughter sent to do?"

He takes a step back, letting his heavy length trail along my nose and over my forehead. It's crude. There's nothing sweet about him rubbing his erect cock all over my face, but I'd be lying if I said I didn't like it.

It's perfect and I want to feel it everywhere. The shaft is velvety soft, yet hard, and the scent of it? It's this musky note that makes me clench with need.

I lick my lips, hungry to taste his salty goodness once more. Yes, I want to make him feel better, but I also need this for myself. I highly doubt he'll forgive this deceit, and if this is the only chance I'll have with the man who haunts my dreams, then I plan on enjoying every damn second of it.

Matthew

This girl. *This fucking girl.*

She's stolen my wallet and right along with it my goddamn soul. Here I have definitive proof that she was sent to trick me. Maybe not the mole I'd originally thought, but to lie to me just the same.

Either way, as I stare at her pouty lips and that sinful tongue trail along the seam, I have only one thought. *Take*. Take from her just like she did me.

And that's just what I do.

"Open," I growl, watching her mouth part and eyes widen in anticipation. "That's right, baby doll. You're gonna fix this. *Make this right.*"

Her father mutters something from the hall, but it's muffled by my heart pounding loudly in my ears.

My body is on sensation overload, but I do my best to take it all in, savoring her wetness as I slowly dip the tip of my hard cock into heaven.

"*She's a gift, Matthew. A precious gift.*"

My knees shake and eyes roll back as she suckles on the swollen head before his words are finally registering.

Fucking asshole. She *is* a gift. A gift that spits out pretty lies and prances around like the goddamn temptation she is.

"I warned you, baby doll." Anger boils deep inside and I can't hold back the punishing thrust. "You're mine. Mine to treasure and mine to punish."

She whimpers as I push forward with another thrust, her gagging on the tip the sweetest sound I'll ever hear.

"Tell Daddy you understand. That you know you've been a bad girl and it's time to pay for your sins." My chest heaves as I watch her nod, her teeth grazing my throbbing shaft, the soft scratch threatening to make me cum right here and now.

And lord, if I thought I was a goner before, I lose all vision when her little hands reach up and around, grabbing onto my ass to thrust me in deeper.

Christ. Her tight throat squeezes the shit out of my cock, sending a bolt of lightning right through my length and up my back. *She's got my whole goddamn body shaking.*

"Matthew? Mr. Crown?" Her father keeps calling from the hall, but I'm too far gone to care.

"*What*?!" I growl, slowly pulling back before gripping her head and shoving myself in deep, pounding into her in sharp methodic thrusts. *Jesus. This feels so damn good.* There's no way I'm letting her go. "You wanted me to take your daughter? Well, I have. I'm claiming her. She's mine. *I'm her Daddy now.*"

He mumbles something, but I don't hear it. It's muffled by Hayley's pretty sounds, her slurping and gagging on my length making my balls drop even lower as they fill with cum.

"That's it, baby. *Choke on it.*" I throw my head back and roar as she sucks in earnest, the little thief swallowing me with every push forward. "*Goddamn.* You might look like an angel, but you suck cock like a whore."

There's a sharp squeak. "Oh god, are you?" Her father's horror registers somewhere in the recesses of my brain, but ask if I give a damn. *I sure as fuck don't.*

Lowering my gaze, I see my doll's swollen lips take me in and I know I need more. Digging fingers deeper into her scalp, I hold her head still as soon as I'm buried deep in that tight as fuck channel.

"*Stay*," I growl, commanding her to take me in and keep me there.

And call me a goddamn degenerate, but my heart swells as she swallows me deeper and her eyes leak with the tears we both feel.

It's bizarre. My heart clenches with the pain of seeing her suffer, but it's in direct conflict with the need to punish her.

I need to take out this ache I have on her throat and show her she's mine—*lies be damned.*

Yes, she might've come into my life under false pretenses, but there's nothing fake about what I feel now. Like it or not, she's stuck with me.

"That's it, baby." I back out slowly, watching her gasp for air as I swipe at a tear. "Such a good girl, making Daddy feel better."

I brush a sweaty strand away from her forehead, letting my cock hang there as I watch streaks of black run down her temples.

"Beautiful. Fucking beautiful, baby."

Hayley gives me a sad smile and I'm about to ask her if she's okay when one of her hands wraps tightly around me, her pretty pout whispering for more, before she shoves me inside, picking up the pace as she gags and chokes with every pull forward.

Fucking hell. I need this, but as she takes me in after a moment of reprieve, I know she needs it too.

If this is her apology, *I'm taking it.*

"*Jesus*, you suck Daddy so good." Hayley whines, her thighs pressing together with need, and I melt. "How could I stay mad at such a pretty little thing?"

I reach down and the action causes me to slip out of her mouth. But like a man on a mission, I forsake my pleasure for a moment and hike up her tattered dress before shoving her thighs wide open.

There it is. All puffy and swollen from the love I'd given it earlier. She's smooth and glistening with need and I know I have to watch her unravel once more.

"This pussy. It's mine too." I give her bare lips a quick slap, thankful we'd left her panties on the bed of my truck. "Now be a good girl and play with it while you choke on my cock."

Her eyes widen as she licks her lips before whispering, "Yes."

"Yes, what?" I narrow my eyes, waiting on the words we both love to hear. And like the good girl she is, my baby delivers.

"Yes, *Daddy*."

Darkness fills my vision as she takes her free hand and guides my length into her mouth, bouncing me in and out, letting me slide into that hot velvet channel every time. *Goddamn*, I'm about to explode.

I know I won't last much longer as my back tightens

and a deep rumble emanates from my chest as the warm wetness of her mouth swallows me whole. "*Ahhhhh, fuck.* I can't. I can't stay mad at my baby."

Inky black envelopes me as liquid heat shoots straight through my hard length and right down my doll's tight little throat.

I'm pulsing rope after sticky rope of hot cum and I know that forever wouldn't be long enough.

In a trance, I watch her fingers furiously circle her clit while her toned little body clenches with the onset of her release. *She's absolute perfection.* And as the column of her throat bobs up and down, her tight little throat drinking me in, I know this is it for me.

Mole. Thief. Liar. *Whatever she is.* She's mine. Every bit of her.

Chapter Sixteen
HAYLEY

IT CAN'T BE OVER. IT JUST CAN'T.

Now that I know what he tastes like, what he feels like in my mouth—there's no going back.

The thought of any other woman having him sends me into blind panic and I can't stop the tears as they pour freely from my eyes.

"Shhh. It's okay, baby." Matthew pulls me up off the bed and lifts me to his chest, and like a little koala, I wrap my arms and legs around him, freely feeding off the comfort he provides. "I'm right here, sweetheart. Daddy isn't going anywhere."

This. This is what I need. To feel safe and secure, knowing he's not going to leave.

With an open palm, he rubs slow circles on my back, and it gives me the confidence to speak. "I'm so sorry. I didn't—"

"Stop. It's okay." He pulls back, giving us enough room so we can look each other in the eye. "I mean it, baby doll. You belong to me, and there's nothing you could do that would ever push me away."

His words crack me wide open and a weight I didn't know I'd been carrying lifts. Is this real?

"But—" I start to ask when I'm interrupted by my father's untimely words.

"So… I take it we're good now?"

My mouth drops open as the realization that he's been outside the room this entire time dawns on me. I'm flushed with heat and embarrassment. I'd been too lost in my desire for Matthew Crown to stop and think of my actions.

It was as if I were on autopilot, needing to feel him, needing to make him feel good.

I'm about to scramble off of Matthew when he pulls me in tighter, letting one of his hands drop as he tucks his delicious cock back inside his pants.

And just when I think I couldn't further die of embarrassment, this man does the unthinkable—he turns and walks out the bedroom door with my body still perched on his.

Oh god. Parker Barclay is gawking, his eyes blinking as

he takes us both in. There's no doubt he knows what transpired behind that door. Hell, if the sounds we were making didn't clue him in, then my tattered dress and ruined makeup surely does.

"Mr. Barclay, to answer your question—No. We are not good now. I doubt we ever will be." Matthew lowers me to his feet before intentionally maneuvering me behind his tall frame. "I don't intend on doing business with a man who barters their own flesh and blood in exchange for profit. It's sick and without reproach. I will, however, keep your daughter. She's mine and no longer your concern."

Father is sputtering now, his face turning beet red. "You can't do that. She's—she," he takes a step toward me, but Matthew blocks his movement. "She fucking owes me! That little brat owes me!"

I bristle at his words, but Matthew's hand in mine gives me the strength and courage I need to finally stand up to this monster. Stepping to Matthew's side, I raise my chin in defiance and speak the words I've so longed to hear.

"No, *Father*. I don't owe you. I was a child and something unfortunate happened. That tragedy came about because of half-truths and lies—lies that weren't mine." I can feel Matthew's intense stare, but I can't face him. Not yet. "So, thank you for the opportunities you've given me, but I will no longer cower and concede to your every whim. I do not owe you a damn thing. Not now. Not ever."

Parker's eyes bulge and that vein on his forehead throbs. "You little—" He's lunging for me when Matthew knocks him clear across the temple, making the monster slam into the wall before crumpling to the ground.

He's out cold, very much like his heart.

I'm still blinking at his body when Matthew's touch on my shoulder makes me jump.

"Hey. You okay?" He's staring at me with so much concern and it makes my heart squeeze.

"Me? I should ask you that. You just found out my father tried to con you, using me as his accomplice. Yet here you are, asking if *I'm* okay?" I let out a sardonic laugh. "I'd be ready to run out the door if I were you."

Matthew purses his lips and raises a brow. "No. You wouldn't. You're just as fucked as I am, aren't you?" He pulls my chest into his body while his arms wrap around me, but I don't speak. I'm still in shock. "Daddy asked you a question, doll. You will answer or suffer the consequences."

This has my mouth parting and breath quickening. "Another punishment?"

Matthew's head falls back as he chuckles. "Oh, I see. I've got myself a horny little thing."

My cheeks heat and I can't exactly deny his statement, so I don't. I give him my truth.

"*Only with you.*"

His eyes lower to mine and I see them fill with wonder. "Damn straight, only with me." Matthew lifts me over his shoulder before stepping over Parker's body and walking into the bedroom. "Why don't you change into something more comfortable? I've got some business to handle."

"What are you going to do with him?"

"Nothing. I'm just going to have a friend take him home, is all."

I nod as he lowers me onto the bed, my eyes drifting back toward Parker's pathetic form. The man who tortured me for the better part of my life seems so small now, laying there in a heap, that I wonder how'd I let him hurt me for so long.

"Hey." Matthew places two fingers under my chin and lifts my gaze up to meet his. "Don't worry about him anymore, okay? I've got you."

And even though his words bring me comfort, there's a part of me that wants me to have my back, too. Yes, it's amazing that I have him in my corner and that he makes me feel safe, but this is something I need to come to terms with on my own.

There's still so much left unsaid. So many things to be sorted out. I sigh, letting out a labored breath. *One day at a time.* This is a long-term battle, and as I look at Matthew, I know there's no one else I'd rather have by my side.

I've finally caught a break, and maybe, just maybe, good things are headed my way.

MATTHEW

"Thank you for coming so quickly." I close the door behind Titus. He's with WRATH securities and here to help me with the mess that is Parker Barclay.

"No problem. I was switching shifts with William over at your brother's ranch." He walks straight past the kitchen before stopping dead in front of Parker's body where I've laid it up on the couch. "*Jesus*. Just how hard did you hit him?"

I let out a sigh and slowly tilt my head back. "I didn't mean to knock him out like that. My fist just happened to connect with his head at just the right angle. And well, here we are."

"What a coincidence." Titus raises a brow. "What do you want me to do with him? Am I sending him to New York? Having him meet the Renzetti brothers or am I—"

"Whoa, whoa. There's no need for all that… *yet*." My eyes narrow as I step around them both, glaring at the poor excuse of a man. "I called you because his daughter shed some light on something I want dug up. Mr. Barclay here thinks his daughter owes him something. She mentioned half-truths and lies. Seems like he's holding something over her head, and we can't have that."

Titus gives me a tight-lipped nod. "Right. Don't want anything he could try to blackmail your girl over. Or you and the family, for that matter." He's raising a brow, a slow smirk pulling at the corner of his mouth. "So, it's true then. The last Crown brother is off the market."

"Oh god, have my brothers been running their mouths again? I swear they're worse than cackling hens."

Titus claps me on the back. "You know they mean well. They're just excited to see you as happy as they are."

A dry chuckle tumbles from my lips. "Yeah, well. That's yet to be determined. She may not be the mole I thought she was, but clearly the Barclays are hiding something."

Titus' face turns solemn. "Whatever it is, you know we'll dig it up."

"I know. That's why I called." It's my turn to smirk, only to be met with Titus rolling his eyes.

There's a sputtering sound, and it appears Mr. Barclay is finally coming to.

"Morning sleepy head." Titus speaks in a sardonic tone. He truly is a creepy fucker, and it's clear Parker thinks so, too. He's shaking like a leaf.

"Who—who are you?" He turns to me before his eyes dart back to Titus. "Mr. Crown? What is the meaning of this?"

He's trying to act all tough, but it's all bravado.

"I'm glad you asked." I wave a hand toward Titus. "This here is Titus. And he's taking you home. You've recently sustained a head injury and the last thing we want is you having another accident."

Parker's brows furrow as he tries to piece things together and it's clear he doesn't trust us one bit. I mean, I don't blame him. I just knocked him flat on his ass not thirty minutes ago. Too bad. He's getting an escort, like it or not.

"Oh. But I hate being any trouble." Parker moves to get up but Titus shoves at his shoulder, forcing him to sit back down.

"It's no trouble at all, sir. I assure you." Titus attempts to smile but it comes out like the Joker's wild grin and it's the opposite of comforting.

Not wanting Parker to piss on my couch, I offer him a modicum of security. "Look, Mr. Barclay. My friend is going to take you home and ask you a couple of questions. That's all. You have my word."

I look at Titus as I utter that last promise, needing him to know he's not to get too knife happy or anything.

He may not be as sadistic as the cartel members, but I wouldn't put a Colombian necktie past him, should the situation call for it.

Parker slowly nods, and I'm glad he's finally warming up to the idea. The longer I stay out here with him, the less time I have with my girl.

"Okay, but just so you know, I'm calling my housekeeper and letting her know to expect me. If I don't show up, she *will* call the police." His beady eyes keep bouncing back and forth between Titus and me, as if we were to pounce on him right then and there.

I roll my eyes and let out an exasperated sigh. "I already gave you my word. Now if you'll excuse me, it's time for you to go."

I nod at Titus who shoots me a Cheshire grin while hoisting Mr. Barclay to his feet, his squeak one I don't care to hear.

"Matthew, you gave me your word!" The man is shaking in Titus' hold.

"That I did," I mutter, walking behind them and toward the door. *"Don't make me regret it."*

Chapter Seventeen
HAYLEY

It's bumpy on the way to the station this morning, and I'm not just talking about the road.

I woke up to an empty bed, feeling lost. Yes, I know we were in my apartment, and yes, I know Matthew gave me his assurance last night that he wasn't going anywhere, but I still can't shake this feeling. As if what we have were hanging by a mere thread.

Ugh. I hate feeling this way.

"You okay, doll?" Matthew glances at me before focusing his attention back on the road.

"Yeah. Just restless, I suppose. Having your friend

interrogated isn't exactly the most calming experience." It isn't a *total* lie. I'm not just worried about myself this morning. Mel is facing some serious questioning.

In a reassuring move, Matthew reaches over and places one of his large hands on my thigh. "Everything is going to be okay. My brothers and I have a plan."

I giggle. "So long as it doesn't involve one of your lock downs, then I think we're good."

This has Matthew pulling his hand back before he's shooting me a look I can't quite decipher.

"And why is that, Hayley? You don't think our lockdowns are any good?"

Oops. I think I've hit a sore spot.

"Look, don't take this personally, but it seems like every time you've had a lockdown, one of the girls—or multiple girls, for that matter—have gone missing. Let's just say it doesn't inspire trust."

I'm shrugging my shoulders and lifting my hands as if to weigh an imaginary scale, but Matthew is far from amused.

"Trust," he snorts, "As if you're one to speak of trust."

My jaw drops as I stare at him blankly. "What is that supposed to mean?"

Both of his hands firmly grip around the steering wheel as his jaw tightens. "You know damn well what I mean, Hayley Barclay."

My father. He must be talking about my father and his stupid plan to play him.

"I thought we'd moved past that last night." I shake my head and sigh. "There was never any intention to seduce you. Well, not once I found out who you really were. In fact, I tried my hardest to stay away from you, but it was you who approached me at the bar first, and it was you who invaded my personal space after that—each and every time."

Silence. I'm met with nothing but silence because it's true, and he knows it.

A beat passes before Matthew answers, "You knew what you were doing with those tight little dresses and that come fuck me stare."

I laugh out loud. "Although I love the fact that you find my modest dresses so alluring, I'll have you know I didn't change into skimpy office attire, despite my father's wishes." My mind flashes to Sara and I want to hurl, jealousy souring my stomach. "It isn't like I was walking around in six-inch heels and mini skirts like your office administrator. She's clearly been trying to bag herself the last available Crown brother."

Matthew's expression softens and a smile slowly spreads across his luscious lips. "I knew you were jealous the moment she laid a hand on me." He chuckles before waggling his brows. "Not gonna lie. It was hot watching you want to gouge her eyes out."

I cross my arms over my chest, not finding this amusing one bit. "Well, next time she tries that, she's for sure losing an eye."

Roaring laughter falls from my man's lips and it's the most beautiful sound I've ever heard. *Seeing him light up with joy like this?* Yeah, I could get used to that.

"Don't worry, baby doll. If she tries that again, she's as good as gone. I'll be sure to let everyone know where we stand as soon as we get back to the office."

This has me inhaling deeply and my heart speeding up a mile a minute. "Uh, what do you mean?"

Matthew grabs my hand and pulls it onto his lap. "I mean that we're both off-limits because you're mine and I'm yours."

My heart is about to explode from how fast it's beating. *Is this real life?* Is the man of my dreams saying he's mine?

I take a centering breath, letting it all sink in.

"Okay." I squeeze his hand back and know that I have to speak my mind, or I'll regret it. "As much as I love the idea of us, we need to get some things straight."

Matthew's brows shoot up, but thankfully his smile doesn't dissipate. "Oh? And what are these things that need straightening?"

Now or never, Hayley. I need to set up boundaries and make my intentions and desires clear. I've had enough tiptoeing around people to last me a lifetime, and I'm not doing it anymore.

"If we're going to be in a relationship then there needs to be trust. We can't have this," I wave a hand between the both of us, "without it."

He's nodding slowly, taking in my words yet refusing to let my hand go. "Okay."

"Okay? Just like that?"

"Yes. Just like that." He gives my hand a little squeeze before his next words have my blood freezing. "You're right. Every relationship needs to have trust in it. So let's throw all of our cards on the table. You go first. Tell me what your father meant when he said you owed him. Why does he think you owe him, Hayley?"

My lips part and I try to pull my hand free, but he isn't having it. He only squeezes it tighter before his next words make my little heart beat right out of my chest.

"I told you, baby doll. I'm not going anywhere, and neither are you. We're forever. Lie, steal, or cheat. I'm keeping you. Might have to murder a few along the way if you did the latter, but I'm fucking keeping you." I'm still speechless when a disembodied voice booms from the speaker.

Incoming call From Spencer—

"Fucking hell. Always with the timing, this one," Matthew mutters as he presses a button on the dash. "Talk to me."

"Hey, how far are you? All hell has broken loose." The sheriff is agitated, and you can hear commotion in the background.

"Christ. What happened?"

"Your brother, that's what happened. How far are you?"

"About five minutes. I need details. *Now*, Spence."

There's a pause before the sheriff whispers, "One of the feds got a little confrontational with Mel. Got a little too close for Hunter's comfort. Personally, I think it was intentional."

"Of course it was fucking intentional!" Matthew roars and I swear the entire truck shakes. "They're trying to get him riled up so he'll attack and they'll have a reason to take him in! My question is why the fuck was he allowed to watch!? I thought we'd agreed that he wouldn't have eyes on the room, that he'd just be in the building."

"Well, you know your brother. There was no convincing him. Hell, the questioning wasn't even supposed to start for another fifteen minutes, but he just had to see the room his girl would be in. Said he had to make sure there weren't any dangerous traps." Spencer snorts. "As if this were some James Bond movie and everyone was out to get his girl."

This has Matthew downright growling. "You say that as if you hadn't lived the past two years right along with us. Newsflash, Sheriff. Everyone is out to get our family, and now that Mel is a part of it, she's wanted too."

Silence settles across the line and I know Matthew's put Spencer in his place, but what good does it do us now? It sounds like Hunter's already in trouble.

"We're here. See you soon. Seems like we have a lot of damage control on our hands." He cuts the line before Spencer has even answered, and I don't blame him. I'm pissed as hell, too.

Matthew finally lets my hand go, but not before placing a soft kiss to the back of it. "Come on, doll. I think Mel could use some comforting right now."

I swoon. Here his brother lies in a heap of trouble, yet he still thinks of my friend's well-being too. I think I could really love this man. *Ha! Who am I kidding?* I think I loved him from the moment he first laid hands on me.

Yup. As far as Matthew Crown is concerned, *I'm a goner.*

Matthew

"Jesus. This is bad. Really bad." I look at my brother and then at the two federal officers, both with black eyes.

"Well, at least it looks like Hunter came out of this without a scratch." Jace chuckles beside me.

"Yeah, for now. Just you wait until they get him behind closed doors. They'll get their pound of flesh then." Spencer grimaces.

I turn to look at the sheriff, and although he may be a big deal around town, it doesn't change the fact that he failed my brother and his supposed friend. "We can't let that happen, and if it does, I'm holding you responsible."

"Me? For fuck's sake, Hunter is a grown man. And you should know better than anyone that once a Crown gets something in their head, there's nobody on this green earth who could deter them."

I let out a frustrated sigh. *He's right.* And if I were being completely honest with myself, I knew that there was no way to come out of this unscathed.

A Crown woman was in the line of peril, and there's no keeping her man from coming to her rescue. And those women? Yeah, they're just as bad.

I turn to look at Hayley and Mila. They're holding Mel back, keeping her from running to Hunter, who's being cornered by the soured officers. Frankly, it's a miracle she hasn't landed a few blows herself.

Focusing back on Spencer, I ask the obvious. "Why haven't they attempted transport yet?"

"I told you. Questioning wasn't supposed to start for another fifteen minutes when all of this went down. They were operating a few men short."

"Yeah. Titus said he's got eyes on the other two officers. They're still at Poppy's Diner."

I rub at my scruff and look toward Jack. "You thinking what I'm thinking?"

Jack nods. "Yup. Already on it. The lawyers are diffusing the situation as we speak."

That's when I see the men in suits. The older one is on the phone. His eyes are intent on my brother.

"Good. Spence, you call Poppy's and see if the gentlemen could be distracted for a few. Just until we get this situation sorted."

The sheriff raises a brow. "Y'all are just lucky that Poppy is working the counter today. That woman can pull anyone into a never-ending conversation. I swear, she's worse than my ex-wife with the incessant chatter."

I wait until Spencer disappears into his office before speaking. It's not that I don't trust him, but this is family business.

"I think it's time."

Jack and Jace nod. "Austin is on his way back from the ranch with the file."

"I figured as much when I saw that he wasn't here. Even though he and Hunter have their problems, I knew he'd come through for him."

Even though it would tarnish the Crown name, if it meant saving our brother, then we'd be more than willing to share our family's secret history with the feds.

"Yeah, I see what you're saying, but I still don't think giving them more dirt on Raul and Catherine is going to change anything. I mean, the man killed his own brother and Catherine practically stole a child, raising it as her own. That should be enough to lock both up."

I sigh, placing a hand on my brother's shoulder. "Raul murdered his brother in Mexico and we don't have any direct evidence of that like we do the paper trail he left behind while working with our father. And as far as Catherine, that point is moot now. Mila is a grown woman and digging all that back up will expose her to unwanted attention. Why would you willingly put your girl on the spot like that?"

Jace groans. "Fuck, you're right. I just don't like the

idea of giving these assholes anything. Especially not something that could put Father in a bad light."

"I know, brother. I don't like it either. But we're in quite the pickle, aren't we?" Jack narrows his eyes on Hunter and the men that are getting a little too handsy.

"Yeah. We sure are. Just as long as we don't give them any information that could implicate Father or Austin in any of the cartel's wrongdoing, then we should be fine."

"That's what the lawyers are for. I'm having them look at the file as soon as Austin gets here." Jack breaks his gaze to look toward the door as the last remaining Crown brother walks in.

"So that's it then? We're just going to give them more dirt on Raul and pray they take the bait so they'll get off of Hunter's back?"

Jack snaps. "Listen, if they take Hunter right now, he's as good as dead. Either by the rogue cartel members in the system or by the feds themselves. This is the lesser of all evils. I don't like it one bit, but it's all we got right now short of having Hunter run fugitive."

"Fugitive? I like the sound of that," Austin quips as he hands our eldest brother the file.

"Doesn't look like he'll have to run just yet." Spencer walks up behind me and I wonder just how much he'd heard. "Just talked to your boy Titus at the diner. Said one of the men tried to get fresh with Poppy. Caught a little unsolicited incident between the two on the way to the restroom."

"Jesus. Is she okay?" My brows furrow and blood boils. If there's one thing I can't stand, it's a man taking advantage of a woman. Yeah, I'm a little aggressive with my girl, but I don't move forward unless I know she wants it. My cock starts to get hard at the memory of her taking me into her mouth and I have to quickly shake myself out of it. *Focus, man.*

"Yeah, Titus caught them just in time. Seems like he had her pressed against a wall and she was scared shitless."

"*Motherfucker*," Jack curses under his breath.

"Well, Titus got footage of it. Footage that could be used as leverage to let your brother go."

Jace snorts. "I swear, those men of WRATH are worth their weight in gold."

"Well, that's about what we pay them. We should just keep them on a constant supply of gold bullion at the rate we call on them."

"Won't get a complaint here." William joins our growing circle of conversation, and as the head of WRATH securities, I sure as hell bet he wouldn't have any complaints with taking payment in gold.

"Hey, at least you'd be worth every bit of it." Jack pats him on the back. "Any word on when Titus will be in with that footage? Also, I think we should have someone cover Poppy. Don't want her to get suicided in an attempt to silence her, you know?"

"On it. I've got one of our men keeping tabs on her.

And as far as the footage? Titus is on his way into the station with the other two officers. Should be here soon."

"*See?* Worth your weight in gold."

William laughs. "Ha! Damn straight. But don't go giving me the accolades until we've cleared your brother of this mess."

"Oh, they'll agree to it." I look at the men with wounded egos and know that they won't refuse our offer. Despite looking like battered housewives, there's no way they'd let one of their own go down.

It's the only thing we have in common—*loyalty*.

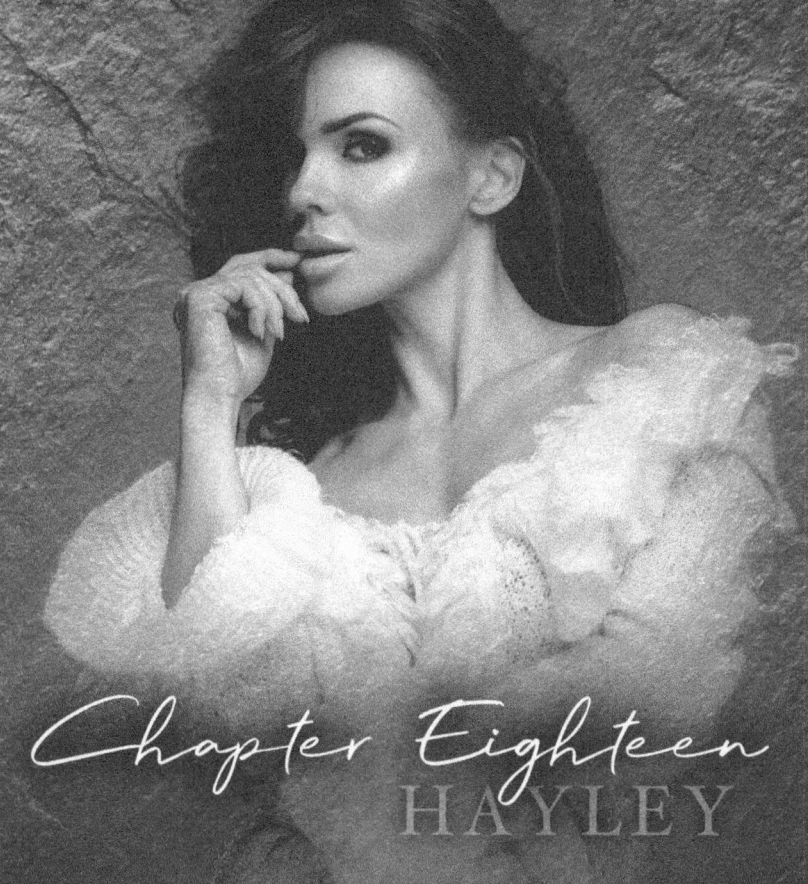

Chapter Eighteen
HAYLEY

"What happened, Mila?" I don't even bother asking Mel who's seemingly in a blind panic.

"One of the officers was a little forward with Mel. He got too close for Hunter's comfort and then all hell broke loose." She's actively holding our friend back, and I'm afraid she won't be able to for much longer. Where Mel is tall and athletic, Mila is short and petite, not to mention her center of gravity isn't the greatest now with her belly at full-term.

"Hey, Mel." I try to get through to our friend, hugging

her to give poor Mila a break. "You're only going to make things worse for Hunter if you storm over there."

This seems to slow our friend down a little, but her spirit dims right along with her will to fight and it breaks my heart to see.

"I know. But I can't help seeing him like that." She swipes at a tear while sniffling. "They can't take him. They just can't."

"They won't. Look." Mila juts her chin toward the men all huddled together. "The guys are working on something, and you know there's no way they'd let them take Hunter."

"Yeah, I think you're right. I bet they'd make a scene and cause a distraction. Anything to let Hunter get away if that's what it came down to." I'm half joking, half not. The more I get to know these men, the more I realize just how fiercely loyal they are—and I'm here for it.

Mel sighs as her body relaxes. "Whatever it takes. I'd even happily go into another damn lockdown if it meant having my man home and safe."

I snort. "Oh god. About that…"

Both women are focused on me, and I know I need to come clean with what's transpired between Matthew and me.

"Yeah?" Mel raises a brow in anticipation.

"You up for a distraction?" I ask, glancing back at Hunter and his two guards.

"Ugh, yes. Please, I don't think my arms have much fight left in them." Mila groans while Mel rolls her eyes.

"I'm not even fighting you anymore. I trust we'll find a way out of this, and if we don't, I'm willing to go down clawing and screaming." Mel turns to me while pursing her lips. "Well? Spill it, girl."

"I think Matthew and me are official."

This has both women squealing and the entire station looking in our direction.

Mila, trying to act nonchalant and divert curious stares, raises both palms. "We're good. Promise."

I snort. *Yeah.* We're definitely inconspicuous now.

Mila shrugs, turning back toward us. "What? I had to do something. They were all staring."

Mel rolls her eyes. "Anyway, go on and give us the details. How'd it all go down? Who caved first?"

I let out a slow breath, thinking back to the very first time we touched. "Geez. I can't really say who caved first. It seems like every interaction was charged from the start."

"I'd say so. That night at the bar, I'm sure you would've let him pop that cherry had you not found out who he really was." Mel purses her lips and my cheeks flush. *She's right.* I so would've.

"Well, he sort of made it official this morning. Said as much anyway, right after I gave him shit for the efficacy of their lockdowns." I roll in my lips and raise both brows as both women giggle.

"You *did not* call their lockdowns ineffective." Mila raises her brows in disbelief.

"I sure did. And I'm still not convinced they're all that great."

"Too bad. You're all in lockdown as of right now." Matthew's chiding voice sounds off behind me and I instantly regret my words.

"Damn. It's like I spoke it into existence." I pout and Matthew chortles.

"I highly doubt it. This has nothing to do with you and everything to do with not wanting the boys over there to seek retaliation on our women." Jack tries to usher us to the door, but Mel isn't budging.

"Oh no, you might've convinced Pen and Anaya to stay back at the ranch, but I'm not going there without Hunter." She's standing tall, her eyes set on her man, and I don't blame her one bit.

Jack sighs. "Pen and Anaya stayed home because Mary couldn't watch all the kids. Hell, you shouldn't even be here, Mila. You're about to pop any day now."

"Pregnancy isn't a disability, you know." Mila scowls while Jace comes to her side.

"No, baby. It sure isn't." Her man is staring daggers at Jack now.

Yes, the Crown men may be loyal but come at their women, and they'd gladly take a brother out.

Just then, the sheriff hands Matthew an envelope, but his eyes are focused on me. *What in the world?* "Here. Before you go."

"Is this what I think it is?" Matthew asks, effectively pulling his attention from me.

"Yeah. It's all I got." Spencer nods just as there's shouting coming from the entrance.

"I need to speak to the sheriff!" *Lord.* I know that voice. "He's here! I know it!"

Father? Oh god, no! Is he going to report Matthew for punching him last night?

I go to grab Matthew's hand but he's quicker than me, his tall frame already walking toward the raging man in question.

"Austin, please keep Hayley back."

"Oh hell, no. That's my father. You can't do that!" I may love Matthew's protective demeanor, but I'm not the biggest fan of it right now.

And just as predicted, Austin steps right in front of me, blocking me from moving forward. "You heard Matt, little one. You aren't going anywhere."

"You've got to be kidding me. You can't just hold me against my will like that."

"She's right, Austin." Mila chimes in from behind him. Her hands crossing over her chest in obvious disapproval.

"It's for her own good. You all act as if it's torture when we're just trying to keep you safe." Austin is shaking his head when Mel does the unexpected.

"Yeah, well, that's not your choice to make. It's hers. She's her own person. And you men keep having to learn that the hard way."

"What—?" Austin goes to ask Mel what she's talking about, but she's already putting her plan in motion. In one swift move, she takes her index finger and wedges it hard against the crack of Austin's butt cheeks. "What the fuck, Mel!?"

Austin whirls around to avoid the poke, giving me enough time to maneuver around him.

"Thank you, babe!" I shout, speeding past them both and toward my father.

"Anytime!" Mel cackles as Austin grabs at his ass.

"You're gonna pay—" He growls, but the rest of his words fade into the background as I reach my destination.

Matthew is towering over my father, an expectant glare painting his features. "Well? What's it gonna be?"

Parker looks toward the sheriff and then back to Matthew. "There's no problem. Never was. Must've been something I ate." He takes a step back with both palms up. "That happens, right? Food poisoning causes hallucinations all the time."

"Sure does." Titus snickers beside Matthew.

"*What in the world?*" I speak, drawing everyone's attention.

"Hayley, my sweet. What are you doing here?" Parker's sugary tone is unnerving and I'm weary of this entire interaction.

"That's exactly what I was going to ask you, *father*." I raise a brow at him before glancing at Matthew who's gone eerily quiet, his face devoid of all emotion.

"I was just leaving, sweetheart. Say, why don't you come with me? We can grab breakfast at the little diner in town and catch up."

My eyes narrow, this whole bit he's putting on completely throwing me off. Never in my entire twenty-one years of life have I ever received a loving word from him, but now I'm suddenly 'sweetheart' and 'my sweet?'

I don't trust it.

"Yeah, that's not happening. Hayley has other plans." Matthew steps in front of me as if blocking me from his vision would make me disappear.

I smile, knowing he's coming from a good place, but this is a battle I'll have to fight on my own.

Placing a hand on his back, I step astride and smile. "Now is not a good time Dad. But maybe sometime soon. That'd be really nice."

I don't fully trust him, but that doesn't mean I wouldn't like to have a heart-to-heart at some point. There are so many things left unsaid, so many questions about my childhood that are left unanswered. If he's actually willing to talk, then I'd welcome it.

Parker just nods, his eyes bouncing back and forth between Matthew and me.

"Very well then. I'll be in touch." And with that, the man I've called father my entire life walks out of the station.

As soon as the front door has shut, Spencer claps Matthew on the back. "You're all free to go. Your attorneys are in possession of the footage from Poppy's and the officers in question have agreed to let Hunter off the hook."

"Someone say my name?" Hunter appears, one hand rubbing at the raw skin of the other. *Jesus.* He really laid into those men; his knuckles are downright raw.

"Couldn't keep your hands to yourself, could you?" Matthew is shaking his head but Hunter only snorts.

"As if you could do better if one of those goons tried to touch Hayley?"

Hunter's words are jarring, but looking at Matthew's reddening face, I'd say he isn't wrong.

Wow. Does Matthew really feel that way about me? Are the girls right?

Goosebumps erupt all over my exposed flesh and it doesn't go unnoticed by my man.

"Here." He takes off his jacket, blanketing me in warmth, and it's not just from the piece of cloth he's draped over me. No, it's his actions—the ones that show he truly cares.

With every day that passes, the surer I am that maybe I was destined for love and joy after all.

Chapter Nineteen
MATTHEW

"William, can you have the ladies escorted to their cars?" I place a hand behind Hayley's back, urging her to follow, but she does the opposite and digs her heels into the ground.

"Oh, no. I have a lot of questions. You're not dismissing me like some errant child."

I laugh. I can't help it. She's so fucking cute when she's fired up.

"No, baby. I'm not dismissing you, and I'll answer whatever questions you have on the way home, but there's some private family matters I have to discuss with Titus first."

This seems to appease my doll, but it doesn't stop the sass she deals my way.

"Okay, but I'm holding you to that." Hayley purses her lips and raises a brow, but ultimately follows the other women out the door. "Don't take too long, I don't want you forgetting what you told my father."

I chuckle, using my index finger to tap at my temple. "Don't you worry. This mind's a steel trap."

She pushes her lips to the side as she disappears through the threshold and Titus pats me on the back. "You've got your hands full with that one."

"And I fuckin' love it." My eyes narrow as I stare at the empty door frame. She's come a long way in the few short months that I've known her.

She was reserved, almost to the point of painfully shy whenever it came to anything personal. But now? She's cursing up a storm, being more vocal with what it is she wants. It's beautiful, knowing that she feels safe enough with me to let her true self shine.

"All right, Mr. Love Struck. Let's get this briefing over so you can get back to your girl." Titus shakes his head in amusement, but I know he goes gaga over his woman back home too.

"What did you get out of Parker?"

"It's Hayley's mom. Apparently teenage Hayley had a tantrum, ran out into the street with her mom chasing after her. Ended up getting hit by a car. It was ugly. She—"

There's shouting outside and my heart stops cold. *Hayley.*

I run as fast as my feet can carry me, rushing to see what's going on and if my girl's in danger.

Fucking Parker. I thought he'd left.

He's yelling at Hayley with a very pissed off William in between them.

"Back up, Mr. Barclay, or I'll be forced to draw my weapon."

"She's my daughter, asswipe. I just want to talk to her!"

"*Enough!*" I roar, rushing toward Parker, my hands reaching for either side of his arms and pinning him to the car next to us. "You will not address Hayley now or ever. If she wants to talk to you, then she'll be the one to reach out. Is that understood?"

Parker's lip curls up in a sneer. "You can't tell me who I can and cannot talk to."

I shove a knee into his groin. "I sure as fuck can. Do I need to remind you of my little envelope? I bet you the men in that building behind me would be real interested in your business dealings, Mr. Barclay. It would be such a shame if the empire you've worked so hard for would crumble, wouldn't it?"

"You wouldn't. It's Hayley's name too. You wouldn't tarnish her reputation like that." His eyes narrow and lips twist.

"That's where you have it all wrong. She'll be a Crown soon. Your name and the connotation it'll carry will no longer be her concern, of that you can be sure."

This cockroach pales beneath my grip, the realization of his position finally dawning on him. "That's right, motherfucker. *I own you.* Now, you'll get in your little car and leave my girl alone, you hear?"

A beat passes, but Parker finally nods in agreement. Thank God. I'm not beyond beating some sense into him.

I slowly release him and not so gently shove him toward his green Jag.

"Matthew?" Hayley's tentative voice has me turning toward her, and what I see breaks my heart.

Her big doe eyes are full of unshed tears and she's trembling behind William. *I can't bear the sight.* Rushing to her, I pull her into me and press a kiss to the top of her head.

"Shh. I'm right here, baby." I rub at her back and curse myself for letting her come out here alone. *I should've known better.*

Pulling back slightly, I look down into her big chocolate eyes. "Now, where's my girl? The one who was ready to rip me a new one?"

The corner of her mouth tugs up in a little smirk. "You want that version of Hayley back?"

I chuckle. "I want every version of you, Hayley. You're mine. Mine to cherish, and that includes the fiery bits as well."

Her face is flushed, her pouty lips parted and inviting, perfect for kissing. I'm about to lay one on her when a whistle pulls our attention.

"*Yo*, lovebirds. We're moving out!" Titus calls from a blacked-out Escalade and I see all the trucks lined up behind him. "We aren't leaving until you're part of the caravan. So, let's hop to it."

I chuckle while shaking my head. "Talk to me like that again and you'll be the one hoppin' to it. I don't give a shit if you give off creepy Joker vibes."

This has Titus breaking out into roaring laughter. "Fair enough."

Guiding Hayley to the passenger side of my truck, I help her up, inhaling deeply as her scent of brown sugar and honey hits me. God, I love how she smells. It's mouthwatering.

"What's going through your mind?" She's looking at me expectantly.

"Baby, if I told you all the things I'm thinking, we wouldn't make it out of this parking lot."

Hayley bursts out laughing. "Hey, I wouldn't mind."

I raise a brow and purse my lips. "You say that now, but I'd definitely mind if Titus got an eyeful of my girl. And there's no doubt he'd be right here, egging us on to get going."

Hayley giggles. "You're probably right."

I drop my mouth open in an exaggerated gesture. "What

is this? My girl admitting I'm right? I might have to check if hell froze over."

I close the door just as Hayley rolls her eyes and smiles. God, I love this. Easy banter and the comfort of knowing that she's mine.

Warmth settles over my chest as I round the hood of the truck when it hits me. *This is it.* This is what I'd been missing all along.

And as I climb into the driver's seat, I know that I'll do everything in my power to keep it.

Hayley

Just when I think I've moved past the fear and insecurities my father instilled in me, he shows up to remind me of just how wrong I am.

"You okay, doll?" Matthew releases one of his hands from the steering wheel and places it on my thigh, his fingers digging into the tender flesh and bringing me a semblance of comfort.

"Yes. A little frustrated that he can still ruffle my feathers like that, but given the circumstances, I'd say I'm far better off than your brother and Mel."

This makes Matthew snort. "That's true, but their hardship doesn't diminish yours." A beat passes, but my man doesn't give up. "Talk to me. What's going on? I would've thought you'd have all these questions lined up for me with the way you were sassing me at the station."

"Thanks for reminding me." I giggle. *Yeah, I was a little sassy.* My eyes drop to the envelope in his jacket pocket and his words come flashing back.

'Do I need to remind you of my little envelope?'

"So, what's in that?" I point toward the documents in question.

He raises a brow in my direction. "Before I answer you, I need you to be upfront with me."

This gives me pause, making my eyes narrow. "What do you mean?"

"Trust. It's a two-way street. If we're doing this, you need to tell me everything you know as well. We can't have *half-truths* or outright *lies* between us."

Is he using my own words against me? I think back to the confrontation with my father last night and those are the same things I accused him of. This isn't a damn coincidence.

He's angling for the skeletons in my closet. The very ones I've never shared with anyone before. *Not even Mel.*

"That's a big ask."

Matthew grins. "Is it? Weren't you saying that we needed trust in our relationship? Seems to me like this is a good place to start. It's clear your father is hell bent on controlling you, and as your man, I can't have that."

His words have my head rearing back.

When he puts it like that, like he's in my corner and has my back, it changes things. *Doesn't it?*

But there's no way I could tell him about my mother. He'll never see me the same way again. I was stupid and selfish, running out into the street like that, putting her life in peril and knowing she'd be chasing after me.

"What's it gonna be, doll? You telling me why your father thinks you owe him?"

And as I stare at his profile, I know I can't let him in. Not yet. Not because I don't trust him, but because I know what I did and what I still hide.

I'm not a Barclay. *I'm the sin. The risk. The liability.*

If I told him as much, not only would he look at me differently, but I'd be putting him in jeopardy too. Father always feared that the truth getting out would tarnish the family name, and if I let myself become a Crown, it'll only bring them shame and dishonor. I can't do that.

So doing something I loathe, I lie. Lie straight through my teeth.

"He's spent a lot of money on me over the years. Education, grooming, and extracurriculars. Had me graduating from high school early just so I could work with him. Said I needed to pay back on his investments." There's a pause, and it's obvious he isn't buying it, so I attempt to give the story some credence. I mean, it isn't a total lie. All of those things are true. "That's why he's had me working at his firm since I turned sixteen. You remember? He told you as much when you were there."

"Hmm." That's it. That's all he says.

Oh god. He knows I'm lying, that I'm holding something back. I can feel it and I bet he does too.

I don't blame him, and I don't dare ask about the envelope again.

I don't deserve to know. How could I when I can't even give him my own truth?

Choosing to change the subject, I attempt small talk. "So, are we going back to my place?"

Matthew grunts, and a beat passes before he finally speaks. "We're driving to Jack's. Don't worry about your things. I'm having them picked up and delivered to the ranch."

I nod, taking in his words. All of them perfunctory, said without a trace of emotion. *Yup.* He doesn't believe me. Worse, I think he's mad at me.

And the sad part is, he has every right to be.

Chapter Twenty
MATTHEW

S*HE'S LYING. I FUCKING KNOW IT.*

I'm watching her settle into the master bedroom in one of Jack's cabins—*our home for the foreseeable future.*

At least until we've sequestered Raul and Catherine. There's no way the feds will get off our back until we do. They need someone to hold accountable and it sure as fuck isn't going to be a Crown.

"You know you can say something. Anything. It's preferable to your following me around like some sentient gargoyle." Hayley turns to look at me over her shoulder before entering the attached bathroom. "You've been silent since we left the station, and it's driving me crazy."

I just grunt. Unable to muster any words for fear of ripping into her. How dare she preach about trust and then turn around and lie to my face?

I'm not stupid. Titus mentioned her mother, and although I haven't gotten the full story, I know it definitely has something to do with why her father thinks she owes him.

"A grunt isn't the same as speaking, Matthew." The little spitfire is back, and she's walking toward me with purpose. *Good.* Maybe she'll finally come clean. Closing the distance, she pokes me in the chest with a finger. "I mean it."

"What do you want me to say, little doll? That I can't see through your bullshit? That I'll gladly pretend like you didn't just feed me lies?"

She's glaring at me now, but I'm not taking a damn thing back.

"I don't know what you're talking about." Her lips part as the tip of her tongue pokes at her cheek. *Yeah, she's lying.*

Ever so slowly, I walk into her, forcing her to step back until she's pinned against the wall. "Baby doll, you can deny it all day, but you and I both know you're hiding something. And eventually I'm going to find out." I run the back of my hand along her cheek before dropping it to her neck, wrapping my fingers around the delicate column.

"Let's just say it'll be a lot easier on that tight little cunt if you come clean now." I squeeze her throat, making her head tilt up and lips part as she looks at me with wide eyes. "Or does my baby need to be fucked into submission?"

Hayley whimpers but doesn't answer, her defiant eyes staring me down.

Taking my free hand, I slide it behind her ass and hoist. "Wrap those legs around me, baby." She does as she's told, her body already arching into mine. "Good girl. Now, if we could get you to trust me with those secrets."

Something akin to panic flashes behind her eyes, and I know we have a lot of work ahead of us. "Look, it's clear you're comfortable sharing your body with me. Why not your past?"

Hayley buries her face into the crook of my neck and her entire body shivers. "I can't. I just can't."

A mixture of anger and hurt hits me square in the chest, a burning sensation occupying every inch of my body.

How could this girl deny me? How could she hold something back when it threatens to destroy us if she doesn't share?

I can't have that. I won't.

"Seems to me like you need a little convincing." I press her firmly against the wall, pushing my groin into her heat and grinding into that hot little slit.

"Matthew," Hayley gasps in surprise, but the rolling of her hips keeps me going.

"What? What does my baby need?" I let the hand that'd

been around her neck drop to her outer thigh, sliding it up, inch by inch before reaching the thin piece of cloth she calls a thong. "What could I do to make you feel better? Safer?"

With one swift pull, I've ripped off her panties, making her legs shake around me.

"Tell me, doll." I drop the lace material before palming her mound, bringing my thumb to her slit. *She's drenched.* Soaked as I stroke up that juicy cunt. "*Now*, Hayley. Tell me."

My girl lets out a whine turned moan as I swirl around that hard little pearl, her nails digging deep into my back. She's a fucking vision as she arches into me, her body trembling with the pleasure I provide.

"*Daddy*," Hayley whines.

One word, that's all it takes and my vision goes dark. I'm a beast. A monster. And I'll take, using every measure possible. *Just or not.*

"I'm right here, baby." I stop my thumb's ministrations just to drag it to her tight little fuck hole, stopping for a beat before thrusting it in and uttering my next words. "Daddy's *right* here. Taking care of his little girl."

Hayley clenches around me and I know she likes what she's heard. *Comfort. Assurance. Ownership.* That's what she needs.

"Don't worry, sweetheart." I keep thrusting as my girl makes pained sounds, but her hips eagerly chase my thumb.

"This virgin cunt belongs to me, and nothing you could say or do would ever make me love it less."

"Oh, God." Hayley throws her head back and her hands clasp onto the nape of my neck. She's hoisted herself onto my fat digit as her entire body contracts around me.

Christ. She's so close with my words and thumb alone.

"I've got you, little doll. Now show me. Show Daddy you trust him." Pulling out, I quickly insert my ring and middle finger at once, pressing the slippery thumb to her swollen clit and rub.

"Yes! God, yes!" Hayley is writhing under my hold, loving the stretch my fingers provide.

"Show me or I'll stop." I raise a brow and slow my thrusting, telling her with my actions I'm not bluffing.

Just then, Hayley clenches around me, as if to keep me there with her grip before denying me once more.

"I can't." She whimpers and I immediately stop. "Please. Don't. I need you. I need this."

Fuck. Her little pout and whining undoes me. How could I deny her? Hell, how could I deny myself?

Lifting her from the wall, I walk us over to the bed, throwing her onto it face first before pressing a hand to her back and holding her there.

"Stay. Only move when Daddy says so. Understood?"

She whines, but nods none the less.

"Good girl. Now, open." I roughly slap the inside of her thighs, and like a blooming rose, she spreads her legs for me.

Not wasting any time, I wrap my hands around her thick thighs, dragging her to me before putting her on her knees and hoisting her ass in the air.

Christ. What a sight.

"Beautiful." Her dress is hiked up around her waist, exposing her smooth cheeks and the valley between. "Look at these pretty little holes, just for Daddy."

Her core clenches before me and it drives me mad knowing she loves the way I talk to her. Crude and raw. There's nothing sweet about it.

Needing a taste, I bend down and press the flat of my tongue against her, running it from clit up to puckered little hole.

"*Fucking delicious.*" I growl into her flesh. "Tell me. Are you ready to give me the truth?"

I thrust three fingers into her cunt, issuing punishing movements as I press the pads of my digits against that magical spot inside.

"*Oh... Oh, God.*"

"That's right, baby. I'll keep this up all night. Starting and stopping until you tell me what I want to hear."

She gasps, pushing her ass into me. "Please. God. No."

"Mercy? Is that what you're beggin' for, sweetheart?" I thrust slower, applying more pressure to the spongy area as I watch her pleasure unfold. "Because you aren't getting any here."

I spit, the slick coating her pink little hole and dripping

down onto my fingers where I continue to slide in and out of her core.

"Punishment. That's what I promised you if you didn't behave, and that's just what I plan on serving you until you tell me what I need to know."

I push a thumb against her rear entrance, but she puckers up tight.

"Now, now, Hayley. It'll be a lot easier if you relax." I circle the muscle twice before stopping to press against it once more. "Come on, baby…let Daddy in."

The magic word has her body softening and my fat finger sliding in ever so slowly. "That's a good girl."

I gently push, waiting until I'm fully seated in both of her holes to ask again. "You trust me, don't you?"

Running the palm of my free hand up her spine and onto the nape, stopping only once I've yanked her hair. "Don't you?"

Hayley whimpers, answering through clenched teeth. "Yes. I trust you."

I press a wet kiss to the small of her back, loving the hiss I hear. She's hungry for more, and she can't hide it. Not with her clenching around me like this.

Slowly, I slide my thumb out before going back in. "Trust me enough to tell me the truth?"

She whines, "I can't." And even though I can't see her face, I know she's pouting.

"Yes." I thrust harder now, moving roughly in and out of both holes. "You can."

"I can't!" She shouts, her hips going wild as she pushes back against me, chasing a release that won't come. Not unless she tells me the truth.

I remove my fingers and Hayley wails. "No! Please!"

"Oh, I'm not done with you." I grab her by the waist and flip her over before ripping off my shirt and dropping my pants. "I'm gonna fuck the truth out of you if I have to."

Her mouth falls open as she drinks me in. This is the first time she's seen me completely naked, and the look in her eyes can be described as nothing but wonder.

"Oh, Matthew."

"No, baby. That's not what you call me. That's not what I am to you." I stroke my hard length, root to tip, enjoying the little lick of her lips as she stares. "That's right, sweetheart. Look at what you've done to Daddy. Made him all big and swollen."

"I'm...I'm sorry." She sounds anything but apologetic as she nibbles on that plump bottom lip, her eyes fluttering closed.

"No. You're not." I kneel onto the bed crawling over her small frame until my hands are at the collar of her dress. With one rough pull, I'm ripping the cream fabric right down the middle. "You're not sorry. But you will be."

She's slack jawed, her gorgeous brown eyes full of heat as I let my hands grope her full tits, squeezing them before I'm slapping the sides and making them bounce against each other.

"Now, are you ready to tell me, or is Daddy going to have to fuck that little cunt into submission?"

She doesn't answer but her legs fall wide open, giving me the room to issue a penance that's more pleasure than punishment.

I lift her ass in the air and place a pillow beneath it, pausing to stare at her beauty. *God, she's gorgeous.* I can't help but grab my turgid flesh and give it a stroke before smacking the angry head against her mound.

"*Fucking it is.*"

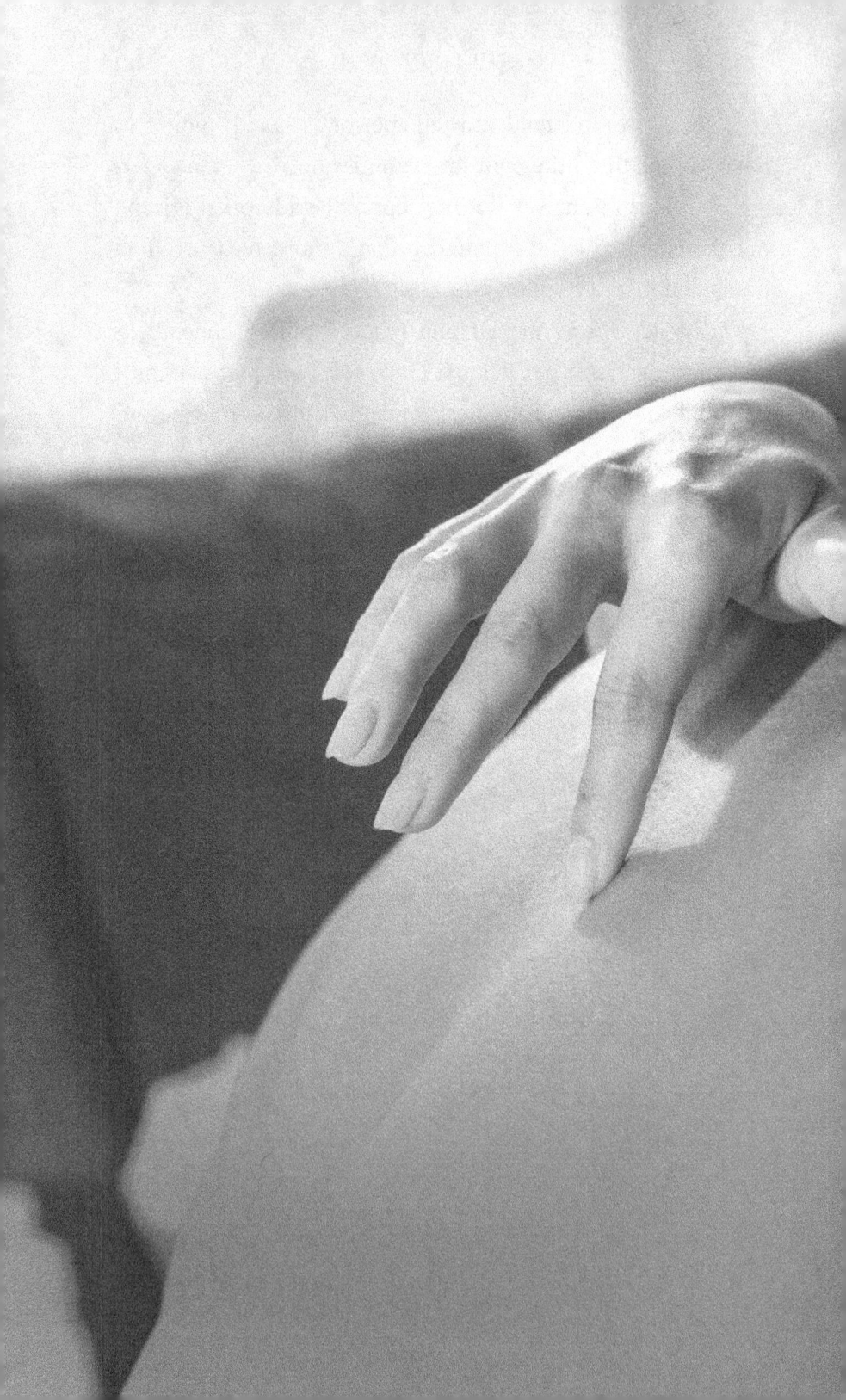

Chapter Twenty-One
HAYLEY

My god. It's perfect. He's perfect.

I'm staring up at his massive length, the shaft thick and long with an angry vein protruding from root to tip. And that tip…. My mouth waters just remembering its taste. *Musky and all man.*

"Now, are you ready to tell me, or is Daddy going to have to fuck that little cunt into submission?"

Oh. My. God. Yes. Please, yes!

I can't verbally answer, but my legs open wide and invite him in. I need this. I need him.

As if in response, he grips my hips and lifts, creating

enough space below to support me with a pillow. And just when I thought I couldn't be any more turned on, he grabs hold of his erection and strokes it. Once. Twice. I'm in a daze as he does the unthinkable. I watch intently as he slaps my pussy with the tip, and *oh my*. I like it.

Matthew's eyes are trained on where our bodies touch, his angry head dragging down between my petals and parting me with his flesh.

My walls clench air. *God, I need him inside*. Looking back up, I see that the inky black of his pupils are blown out, his lips licking in anticipation.

I'm distracted by his beauty, my body shaking with need, when he dips the tip of his length inside. "Fucking it is."

Oh god. It's so filthy, the way he talks to me. The way he touches me. *And I love it*.

"Tell me, baby. Do you want this? Do you want Daddy's cock?"

I worry my bottom lip, trying to lift my hips and take more of him in but he pulls back.

"Words, doll. I need your words." His lower lids flex and a hint of concern flashes behind his eyes.

"I... *I want this*." It comes out barely a whisper and I wonder if he's understood.

Matthew's hand shoots out before his strong fingers are gripping my jaw. "I'm going to need you to be a little surer than that, sweetheart. I may be an asshole, but I would never take what's not freely given." He raises a brow, letting his other hand guide his hard flesh to my slit before rubbing the tip up to my clit and circling.

"*Oh god,*" I moan, unable to hold back the explosion of fire in my core.

"That's a start." His dark chuckle has me opening eyes I didn't realize I'd closed.

He's so damn gorgeous. His hard chest and toned abs need to be touched, so I do. Letting myself act on feeling, I lift both palms and run them down his pecs and washboard abs.

My core clenches at the sheer masculinity before me. He's the epitome of virile and I need him inside, giving me his seed.

Like a woman possessed, I demand he claim me, lifting my thighs to press the back of my feet onto his bare ass. *Jesus*. Even his ass is firm.

I push him to me, urging him to fuck. "Take me, Daddy. I'm yours."

"*Baby.*" He lets another inch slide, my tight walls giving him resistance. "Trust me. I want to pound that pink little hole. But you've gotta tell me you understand. That your secrets—*all of them*—are safe with me."

He pulls back out, and I want to cry. Especially as his hands firmly grip onto my hips, keeping me from thrusting back in. "Tell me you understand, Hayley."

He gives me a little squeeze, urging an answer. And I know he won't move forward until I do. But I'm not ready. It's not that I don't believe him or that I don't trust that he'll want me just the same. Not after everything he's shown me.

No. At this point, it's me wanting to protect him. To keep him free of the shame that surrounds me.

"Look at me, Hayley." He grips my jaw and brings my eyes to his. "This thing between us, I want it to be real. I want it to last, and that won't happen if we don't have trust."

I worry my bottom lip, but he reaches up with one hand and pulls the crest free.

"I mean it, baby. I'm here, no matter what."

My eyes fill with tears as I give him a sad smile. "I know. I believe you. I trust you"

He cradles my face with his hand. "You trust me with everything? Body and soul?"

Justifying it the only way I can, I give him what he wants to hear, despite it only being a partial truth. For now, I can pretend. Pretend that he's truly mine, and that what we have is real.

"I trust you with everything." I push my face into his palm, knowing that it still doesn't change a thing.

"You sure?" He pulls completely out, holding his length in one hand as he repeatedly smacks my hood with his cock.

I moan, arching my back and seeking more. *Torture. This is fucking torture.*

My entire body trembles as he goes from slapping my

clit to tracing my folds with his weeping cock, one of his hands kneading and slapping at my breast.

Never have I wanted anything more than I do this man. I want him inside me, filling me up and stretching me out.

"Yes. Yes, I'm sure." My hands fly to his chest, fingers scratching down his toned abs. "Please. Fuck me, Daddy. I need you."

Matthew growls, "Daddy's right here, baby." And without mercy, he thrusts his full length into my tight-as-fuck pussy, the pressure so strong that I can't help but cry. "*My god*. There's no going back now." He grips my waist as he settles inside, my walls pulsing as they grow accustomed to his fullness. "Doll, there's no way I'm giving this up."

I look up at him, my eyes full of unshed tears. "You promise?"

His words paired with his claiming, it's almost too much. All my life, I've felt unwanted. Like a burden for those around me to bear. Yet here he is, wanting to love and care for me, no matter what. It's too good to be true.

"I promise, baby." One of his hands trails over my sternum before stopping over my heart. "I'm taking care of this." He then lowers his hand to my mound, his thumb swirling over my little button and making me jump. "And this. Forever and always, little doll."

"Oh, Matthew." I cry, pulling him to me and gyrate my hips, urging him to move. I need to feel him, have his body consume me. And even then, it won't be enough. "I love you. God, how I love you."

"*Fuck.* I love you too, baby." Bliss. It's the only word that can describe how it feels to be owned by this man. He's on his forearms, his lower body slowly pulling out before grinding back in, and I can't help but squeeze my legs around him, wanting more.

Slow and intentional. His movements have the tickle in my core rising, my entire body vibrating as he thrusts up, hitting a spot that makes me go blind. *"Holy shit."*

"Does my baby feel good?" he whispers into my neck, but I can't answer. My whole body is on the verge of something far beyond this earthly plane. "Answer me, doll." Matthew bites my neck, his mouth suctioning the tender flesh before releasing it with a pop. "Or Daddy's gonna make you pay."

Oh yes. I want to pay. The price is always delicious. Wanting the repercussions, I remain silent.

"I warned you, baby." Sure enough, my gorgeous man delivers. Lifting his chest from mine, his hands go straight to my breasts, his hands roughly kneading before he's plucking the pointed nipples. "Hands on the rails."

I do as he says, raising my arms above me and gripping onto the iron slats along the headboard. "What are you gonna do?"

With a raised brow, he quickly slaps at the side of my breasts. "I'm gonna start with these tits." He slaps them again before my pussy is left bereft of his cock.

"No!" I whine, needing him back inside.

"I warned you, little one. Misbehave and suffer the consequences." He's crawling over my waist, straddling me as he pushes my breasts together and sliding his length between. "Look at these fat tits, so hungry for Daddy's cock."

Oh my god. It's downright pornographic the way he spits on my perky mounds, the natural lube making him slide up and down so easily that his tip bumps against my chin with every thrust. I can't help it. I open wide on his next push, making him roar as I close my lips around the tip.

"*Fuuuuuuck.* You're goddamn perfect." He keeps himself there as I suck on his head, milking the precum and reveling in its takes. "My perfect little whore."

I softly nod, letting him know that I love being everything he needs. I don't give a shit if others might find this repulsive. I'm done caring about everything that doesn't serve me. New and improved Hayley takes what she wants. And right now that's my Daddy's cock.

"Baby, keep this up and I'll blow my load all over that pretty face."

I whimper, the thought of him painting me with his cum making me see stars. I pull my head back, letting his hard length fall out of my mouth.

My lips part and I beg for it, beg for what I want. "*Do it.* Make me dirty."

"*Christ.* You really are my filthy little whore." He

shakes his head in disbelief as his eyes glisten with wonder. "No, baby. As much as I want to cum on that gorgeous face, I'm not through with your punishment."

Adrenaline rushes through me, my mind racing with ideas of what's to come. "What are you gonna do to me?"

"I'm marking you. Painting your womb with my seed." He positions himself between my legs once more, and my entire body flushes with his words. "This pussy is mine, and there's not a soul on this earth who'll dispute it once you're swollen with my child."

Ohmyfuckinggod. New kink unlocked. Playing along, I feign a pout.

"No. Stop." I slap at his chest, but there's no genuine force behind it. "You can't do that, Daddy. What'll people think?"

His nostrils flare and jaw clenches. "That you're mine, *and they can't have you.*"

I go to speak, but Matthew shakes his head. *"You're. Mine."*

On a grunt, he impales me with his full length, but unlike before—there's nothing slow or gentle about his movement. *No.* This is a claiming. A man rutting into his girl and owning every bit of her soul.

"*Matthew!*" I keen, my chest heaving as I grip onto the rails for dear life. He's fucking me hard, my body bouncing up with every pivot of his hips—and God, how I fucking love it.

"That's it, baby. Call out to me. Let the world know who owns you, who owns this little cunt."

"You do! You *so* do!" *Yes. I want this.* I want to feel him dripping out of me, the knowledge that I could be pregnant with his child urging me on. "Fill me up! Get me dirty!"

I'm on the verge of cresting, my entire body trembling in his hold when he slaps at my tit. Once. Twice.

"Say it, baby. Say you want Daddy's cum."

"Yes. Yes, give it to me. Make me yours." I whine, my vision going black as he applies pressure to my womb. *Black.* I see nothing but black, as pure electricity consumes me whole. I'm shaking, my toes curling as an explosion unlike any other detonates inside me.

I'm still cumming, my walls clenching and releasing around Matthew's length when I feel him pulsing inside, his sticky spend setting off yet another wave of extended pleasure. *Oh god.* I don't want this to stop.

"That's it, baby. Cum all over this cock. Show Daddy how much you love him."

I'm trembling, his words slowly registering as I come off this high. "Yes, I love you. I love you so much."

"Good. Because I love you too." He slowly pulls out, but his eyes remain on where we're joined. "*Christ.* Such a pretty cunt, full of Daddy's spunk."

His words make me blush, but I love them just the same. In fact, I think I've needed them.

Matthew's unabashed ownership makes me feel safe

and loved. Something I know I'll never feel again, not after he finds out I'm not sharing all my truth.

And as expected, reality comes crashing down when Matthew lies beside me, his arms wrapping around me before pulling me to his chest.

A beat of silence passes, and I wish we could stay in this moment forever.

He traces a finger up and down my arm before starting on the inevitable. "I know it can't be easy airing our secrets. But I'm glad that you trust me, doll."

I'm still. Barely even breathing. "Yeah, about that…"

Matthew's hand freezes.

"Oh, no." I'm being flipped around and have no choice but the face the man I love. "You said you trusted me, Hayley. With everything."

Matthew follows me as I sit up on the bed. "I do trust you with everything, but it's not about that. I don't want the dark cloud that's been following me all my life to cloak you in darkness, too."

"The irony." He throws his head back and scoffs. "My family has their own share of drama, and I swore I wouldn't drag another woman into its mess. So I get it. I truly do. But here's the thing. I think you're worth battling life for, because a world where you're not by my side is not a world worth living in."

If it were just the shame of being a bastard child, then that'd be one thing. But there's so much more to my twisted path. I'm a product of the black market, and the evidence that lingers is like a time bomb waiting to go off. There's no way I'd put that on Matthew.

"I doubt you'd think that if you knew all of the ugly that hides in my past." I snort, laughing in self-deprecation.

But Matthew's jaw clenches, and it's obvious he doesn't find what I've said funny. "Hayley, I've already told you. There's not a damn thing you could do or say that would ever push me away."

"You say that now, but—" I'm in the middle of countering his statement when there's a knock on the door, making Matthew curse under his breath.

"Yo, Matt. Round-table in my office." Jack's voice cuts into the tense moment and all I get is Matthew's back as he turns to put on his pants.

I'm thinking he's going to leave without saying anything, but he turns while throwing on his shirt. "This isn't over, Hayley Barclay. Not by a long shot."

And as he pulls the door open and steps into the hall, I know it has to be. I'm not a Barclay and I'm definitely not destined to be a Crown.

Chapter Twenty-Two
MATTHEW

"I'm sorry, brother. I didn't mean to interrupt." Jack looks apologetic, but if I were being honest with myself, he did me a favor. I'm not sure what I would've said had Hayley kept lying to my face.

"Don't worry about it. Let's get this meeting going." *Anything to get my mind off the little siren who's stolen my soul.*

Nope. I'm denied that, too.

"At least you can cross off Hayley on the sus list." Jack chuckles, clapping a hand on my back as we enter his office, but I don't laugh. "Oh, no. Have we changed our mind a*gain*?"

He's staring at me, his frame blocking me from moving further into the room.

"Maybe. Hell, I don't know." I run a frustrated hand through my hair. "She's hiding something. What it is, I have no fucking clue. But it's definitely something, and I can't help but feel that it's somehow tied to everything."

Jack shakes his head but finally moves out of my way, and I gladly step from under his penetrating gaze.

"Maybe you're right." Jack's words have my hackles rising.

It's odd. I'm okay being the one with doubts, but as soon as anyone else tries to paint her in a bad light, it's like this protective beast inside of me comes out, rearing for a fight.

Hunter notices the shift in my demeanor and immediately raises his palms up. "Hold up. Let's just look at the facts. Spencer told us her father is dirty, but that none of his dealings have anything to do with cartel business."

I nod. "Right. As far as he can tell, the paper trail doesn't lead back to the dynamic duo."

"Okay. So let's say, just for shits and giggles, that Raul and Catherine were privy to the same information we are..."

"What? You think they're blackmailing her dad? Having him spy on your company?" Jace asks, brows furrowed.

"But what would be the point of that?" Hunter asks, seemingly just as confused as our youngest brother, even though I think it's pretty damn obvious.

"Leak information. Plant evidence. Maybe they think I have the keys to all of *El Jefe's* assets. The possibilities are endless with the type of access she has to me."

"I'm the biological son. If anyone would have that, it'd be me." Austin scrubs at his jaw, as if he didn't already know he does, in fact, have those damn keys.

He has the keys, the will, the deeds. *Fuck.* He even has the damn gold bullion his degenerate father stashed away for a rainy day.

"Maybe they think it'd be too obvious. Besides, Raul had already ransacked you before he took Pen and Anaya down to Mexico. A narcissist like that can't comprehend that he missed the mark. Surely, he's just moved on to the last Crown brother."

All this is making too much sense, and it's all pointing back to my Hayley being used as a pawn in this sick and twisted history with *El Jefe's* cartel. I don't like it. *I don't like it one bit.*

"So what now?" Jace rubs at his forehead as worry mars his face. "Do we go about proving Hayley's connection, or do we simply hire more eyes on Catherine and Raul?"

"Both," I say definitively. "As much as it pains me to do, I think it'd be stupid of us to turn a blind eye to the very real possibility that Hayley's the mole."

Jack slowly nods. "If that's what you think is best, then that's what we'll do."

Hunter groans, knowing he's going to catch hell if we have to implicate his girl's best friend. "And how are we going to go about doing all of this?"

I rub my lips together, hating what I'm about to say and do. "Leave the Hayley part up to me. I'll get her to come clean. Even if it comes down to torture."

Jack hisses, knowing very well what I'm capable of. "If we have to resort to that, I think it's best we let the men of WRATH handle it."

"*No!*" I roar. There's no way I'd let any other man lay their hands on her.

"See, there's the dilemma. How do you intend to torture her when the mere thought of her coming into danger makes you see red?" Austin raises a skeptic brow.

"You just focus on getting more eyes on the disappearing duo. Leave Hayley up to me." Truth be told, I have no fucking clue, but if I have to edge her, giving her pleasure and withholding release over and over until she comes clean—*then that's just what I'll do.*

Will it kill me to turn her in after the fact? Yes. Will I still do it? Yes.

Nobody sins against a Crown. *Not even my little doll.*

HAYLEY

I'm dying. I'm sure of it.
At least that's what I feel like.

I hate lying in general, but lying to Matthew hits me on a whole new level. Technically, omitting isn't outright lying, but in my book they're the same.

Maybe I should come clean. Tell him about Mother.

Panic floods me, my palms going all sweaty and my skin clammy. *No. I can't.*

"Earth to Hayley." Mel's voice registers somewhere in the recesses of my mind, but it isn't until I'm physically being shaken that I come to.

"Hey." I blink my eyes a few times before they re-focus on everyone in the room.

"Hey to you, too." The corner of Mila's lips turns down. "What's got you drifting out like that?"

"Do I need to go smack a certain Crown brother?" Pen shakes her head in disapproval, as if she has to do this regularly.

This makes me laugh, and I'm thankful for the small reprieve.

"No. No. This is all my doing. If you're going to smack anyone, it should be me." I groan, letting myself fall back into the plush sectional.

"Oh, no. What happened?" Mel sits beside me, her hand reaching out for mine. "You two looked so perfect together out by the station."

Perfect. I laugh sardonically. As if someone with my history could ever be perfect for anyone.

"Let's just say Matthew wants something from me I'm not ready to give."

Anaya gasps. "That filthy Crown. Is he trying to force himself on you? Because if that's the case, I can assure you, the other brothers will set him straight."

I quickly raise my hands, palms exposed. "No! God no!"

Yes, he might be rough and crude, but I love the way we are in the bedroom.

"Then what is it?" Mel's brows push together, a deep crinkle settling in between.

"There's a secret," I whisper, as if saying it any louder will unleash its truth.

Mila pushes her lips to the side, her eyes narrowing. "We all have secrets, Hayley. Whether it was before coming into this family or as we became it."

Mel pats my hand. "She's right. If anyone can understand a sordid past, it'd be a Crown."

I know they mean well, and that they truly believe what they're saying, but they don't know who I really am. They don't know what I've done.

"I get what you're saying. I really do, but there are some things that could never be forgiven. Debts that could never be repaid."

Mel sighs. "Oh god. This better not be about your father and what you think you owe him. I've already told you that wasn't your fault, Hayley."

But there's so much more to that. So much she doesn't

know.

I close my eyes and fight the pressure that's building behind my lids. *I cannot cry. I will not cry.*

Pulling my hand free, I come to a stand, unable to discuss this any further.

"You can't run away from it, Hayley." Pen's eyes are apologetic, her smile sad. "If there's anything I've learned, it's that the truth always comes out."

Mila nods. "Yup. I don't know what it is you think you're hiding, but if it's as bad as you make it sound, then it's best if he heard it from you first."

She's right. I know she is. I just don't like it.

It doesn't matter, though. The ladies are right. This has to end. I need to come clean and confess my sins. I'd be cheating both of us if I didn't.

Matthew is a grown man. It's his choice whether or not he wants to put himself in the line of fire. And as for me, part of being stronger—more confident—is being able to stand alone. If he doesn't want me after what he's learned, then he isn't the man for me.

I'm doing it. I'm coming clean. For me. For *Bad Bitch Hayley 2.0.*

Chapter Twenty-Three
HAYLEY

Standing outside of Jack's office, I debate whether to knock. I'd hate to interrupt their meeting, but I really need to talk to Matthew. I don't like how we left things, and if I lose the little courage I've mustered, I might not fess up after all.

Wait… *Did someone just say my name*?

"So what now?" It's the brother named Jace. "Do we go about proving Hayley's connection, or do we simply get more eyes on Catherine and Raul?"

What the fuck? Connection to what?

Matthew speaks, so sure in his tone, and my heart shatters with his words. "Both. As much as it pains me to say, it'd be stupid for us to turn a blind eye to the very real possibility that Hayley's the mole."

I'm blinking away the disbelief. *He thinks I'm the mole?* I gasp, unable to catch my breath as a deep ache fills my chest. *He does. He really does.*

This all feels surreal. Like a nightmare I can't wake from.

Memories flood me as I stumble back. His touch. His kiss. His vows of concern and possession. *Oh, God. That was all fake.*

My knees wobble before I come crashing to the ground.

And as if I weren't already on the verge of desolation, the man that I love, the man of my dreams, he utters words I never thought I'd hear.

"Leave the Hayley part up to me. I'll get her to come clean. *Even if that means torture.*"

Torture.

That last word loops in my head like a broken record.

I'm in a daze and I'm no longer able to hear the words being spoken in the other room. They're muddled with the pounding of my stuttering heart.

He knows I'm hiding something; he just doesn't know what. And clearly, he's thinking the worst of me, accusing me of being a fucking mole.

How?

My chest quickly rises and falls as I try to catch my breath.

All this time. All this time, I thought he truly cared. *Can you really blame him?* A part of me asks, and I have to really wonder. I haven't exactly been transparent, and I know that could breed doubt. *But this?* To think that I'd be capable of hurting him or his family?

The clacking of heels breaks into my thoughts, and I quickly rise to my feet, wiping away a stray tear. I can't let anyone see me in this state. They'll only ask questions, and I'm nowhere near ready to talk about what I've just learned.

I'm still smoothing down my dress when the last person I'd expect to see rounds the corner.

"Sara?"

She's dressed just as scandalous as ever. We're about the same height, but she's got these platform heels that make her tower a good six inches above me. And lord, her skirt couldn't be any shorter.

She's balancing a massive box, and if she tilts forward just a bit, she'd be mooning everyone within a ten-mile radius.

"No, it's her royal majesty," she snorts. "Anyway, I'm here to see Mattie."

She looks at the door behind me and it's clear she knows the lay of this house. Fire burns in my belly at the thought of her here with my Matthew, but I quickly quash it.

He isn't my anything. He thinks I'm evil, only feeding me his lies to prove that I was the mole. Yeah, I might've come into his life because of my father's shady wishes, but I carried none of them out.

"Ok. This is awkward. Look, I just need to drop off the stuff he asked for." Sara raises a brow as she tries to step around me.

"He isn't in there. They've all left." I think on my feet, trying to piece together a plan, but if Sara's arched brow is any indication, I don't think she's buying it.

"Mary just told me he was in his brother's office." She's pursing her lips, her face resembling that of a constipated stripper.

"Well, they're not. He's not." A beat passes before it hits me. This has to work. "*Buuuut*, I do know where Mattie's private cabin is. It's a short ten-minute drive from the main house." This has her attention, so I keep going. "You drove here, right? I could take you there myself."

"Can't you just tell me where it is? I won't get lost." It's clear she doesn't want me encroaching on her time with Matthew.

Ha! No worries, sweetheart. You couldn't pay me enough to be alone with him. Not after what I just heard.

"Look, Sara. I promise it's better if I go with you." I lick my lips, my mouth as dry as sandpaper, hating what I'm about to say—but it's necessary. "See, if we both go, then I can drive your car back to the main house once you're there. You can tell Matthew I had an emergency or something and you could wait for him all by your lonesome."

I waggle my brows suggestively and it doesn't take long for the thirsty bitch to catch my drift. Oh, she's all about it with the way she's practically foaming at the mouth.

"So, you'd leave?" Her small smile turns into a full grin as I nod.

"Yup. Sure will." I'm already walking around her. There's no way she'll shoot me down. "Come on. The sooner we get there, the sooner you can start waiting on Matthew."

Sara's heels clack rapidly behind me. "You know. I might like you after all."

At least one of us does. I hate lying, but for someone who despises deception so much, I sure have been doing a lot of it lately.

Whatever.

Old Hayley got trampled and abused. But new Hayley? *She isn't having any of that.*

Matthew

It's been a long fucking day and I'm so ready to be home. Well, home here on the ranch.

Hayley and me have taken up in one of my brother's a-framed cabins and if we were staying here under any other pretense, it'd be downright romantic.

The place has massive picturesque windows overlooking a peaceful creek with a cloud-like sectional situated perfectly to watch the water drift on by.

I open the door and I'm greeted with the view, but not the girl. It was too much to hope for that she'd be sitting there waiting for me when I returned.

No, our future isn't one of leisurely mornings sipping coffee after wild fucking. It's more like life behind bars and getting drunk to numb out the pain.

My heart sinks at the realization that I'm about to betray the woman I love. But fuck, she betrayed me first.

I shake my head as I walk to the bedroom. Maybe, just maybe, I could have one more night with her where it's just us. No messed up past or future plotting in the way.

The more I think it over, the better it sounds.

I want to crawl into bed with her and pretend. Pretend that she really loves me and that she's really mine.

The door creaks as I step inside the dark room. The only light is the moonlit glow, but it's faint enough to make out her form under the covers.

There she is. My Hayley.

I eagerly undress, ready to steal this moment and savor every second. I need to feel her, hear her sweet words declaring she's mine—*even if it's all a lie.*

Not soon enough, I pull down the covers and crawl under, pulling her body close.

But something's wrong. Very wrong.

Her scent isn't of brown sugar and honey. *It's floral.* And her curves, they're not as soft. *What the fuck?*

I'm about to say something when her ass presses up against my cock. "Mattie, I knew you'd come around."

"Sara?!" Horror. It's the only description for what I feel, my tensed body retreating as I stumble out of the bed. "What the fuck are you doing?! Where is Hayley?!"

Confusion mars her face before her scrunched features turn into a scowling depiction of fury. "Hayley!? You thought *I* was *Hayley*?!"

"Of course I thought you were Hayley. Why else would I be crawling into bed with you?!" I'm shouting now, something I've never done with Sara, but what in the world was she thinking?

"Because I thought you'd finally come to your senses, Matthew!" And as she calls me by my first name for the first time, I get it.

She crawls off the bed, standing there with nothing but her birthday suit on and, yup—I definitely get it now.

"Look," I sigh, rubbing at my forehead. "I've never been interested in you like that, Sara. You've been my office admin since the start of Tortured Crown whiskey, but that's it. And to be honest, I'm not sure you'll be able to stay on with us. Not after this."

I wave a hand between us, my eyes trained on hers. There's no chance in hell I'm looking down. To be fair, I don't think I'd enjoy it anyway.

Sure, she's pretty. But she isn't Hayley and since I laid eyes on the little thief, my cock hasn't gotten hard for anyone else.

"But you don't even know her." Sara's brows drop and her bottom lip wobbles. "And you asked me here. You asked me to get the files from your home office and bring them to you."

"Here, wrap this around yourself. Last thing we need is Hayley walking in and finding you like that." I pull a throw blanket off a chair and hand it to her behind my back. "And yeah, I asked you because my secretary was out of town and you're the only other person with access to my spare keys."

I hear her scoff as she steps around me. Thankfully, she's wrapped up and her tits are no longer hanging out.

"Well, for your information, Hayley isn't here. Couldn't get out of here fast enough if you ask me." She walks over to the dresser where there's a large brown box before knocking it over, like a petulant child. "Here's your *stuff*."

I'm still stuck on the fact that she said Hayley wasn't here when I see it. My fucking wallet sitting atop all the files I'd asked her to bring.

Rushing over, I pick it up, inspecting it like it's some foreign object. "What's this?"

"Your wallet, *duh*." Sara rolls her eyes as she pulls the throw blanket tighter around herself.

"But... where'd you get it?" My chest hurts just looking at it. God, could I've been wrong?

Sara huffs, but finally answers. "I found it behind the bar. Thought you might've dropped it, so I picked it up and put it in the box before coming here."

Fuck. I *was* wrong. So wrong. Hayley never stole my wallet. She wasn't a thief. Hell, does that mean I'm wrong about her being the mole, too? Of course it does, and deep down I've known it all along.

Shaking my head clear, I drop the damn thing as if it's burned me. "You said Hayley isn't here. Where is she? Back at the house?"

My mind races with all the things I should've done differently. I need to fix this. Make it right with my girl.

"How should I know? She bolted as soon as I gave her the keys to my car."

We're walking out into the living area when Sara's next words send a chill up my spine. "Oh my god! That whore took my coat!"

I close my eyes and let out a slow breath before fully facing my now former admin. "Let me get this straight. Hayley couldn't get out of here fast enough. She took your keys. She took your car. And she took your coat."

"Yes, Matthew. I never took you as dense. That's what I've been saying all along." Sara rolls her eyes for the millionth time. "Obviously, the girl doesn't want you. And now, I don't want you either."

Bile crawls up my throat. She's gone. I just know it. Hayley is no longer here, and this bitch thinks I'm going to be twisted up about the fact that she's no longer pining over me? *Grow the fuck up.*

"Put your clothes on, Sara. We're leaving. *Now.*" I don't have a second to spare, but I definitely don't want to leave her behind. Lord knows what a woman scorned will do.

"Sheesh. I'm going." She drops the blanket and I whirl. Not wanting to see her little show.

"You have two seconds, or I'm leaving your ass behind." I'll just have one of the men on the security team come get her.

"No! No! I'm ready." She rushes by me, heading straight for the door. "This place doesn't even have cable. No way I'm staying here. I'd die of boredom."

Of course she'd think this place was boring. Yet another reason why we were never a good match.

No. The girl for me is long gone, and I might as well have been the one to drive her away.

Chapter Twenty-Four
MATTHEW

"What do you mean she drove right out?!" My ears are hot, and I can feel the vein in my neck pulsing violently.

"She had Ms. Humphries' vehicle, sir. They have similar hair color, and with wearing the same coat and large sunglasses…" The man who'd been posted at the gate shrugs his shoulders. "It was an honest mistake."

Jack places a calming hand on my shoulder, but it's far from soothing. "Attacking our security won't bring Hayley back, brother. And ripping him to shreds won't change what's happened."

He's right. Although it'll feel real good, it does nothing to bring my girl home. But it doesn't mean I'm any less pissed. "Not only is this unacceptable, but it's also extremely dangerous for Hayley."

My thoughts flit back to her psychopath father and the feds who are on our ass. Not to mention Raul and Catherine. *Christ.* She's a shiny new target.

My throat gets tighter and the walls around me feel like they're closing in when Jack speaks. "Right. It isn't safe, so we've got men trying to get her location. She was last spotted at the gas station on the outskirts of town. They've got her on surveillance heading north."

This has my brows pushing together. "North? She has nothing up there. Her house is just over the bend and my place is two hours south."

Someone snorts, and I turn to see who it is. Mel is standing in the hallway, her head shaking and lips pursed to the side in disapproval. "As if she'd want to go anywhere near you or your things."

My eyes narrow as I take two steps forward, only to stop cold when Hunter gets between us. Speaking past my brother, I direct my question toward Mel. "You know where she is, don't you?"

"No." Her lip curls in disgust. "But if I did, there'd be no way in Hell that I'd tell you."

"Hunter." I push at my brother. "You better get your girl to talk."

He pushes me back, our eyes locking. "She told you already. She doesn't know where she is."

"Oh yeah? Then why is she looking at me like I'm the one who ate the last of Mary's cake? She definitely knows *something*."

This has Hunter's brow raising, his body slightly angling toward his girl.

"*Punkin*... Is Matthew right? Do you have any info on Hayley?"

Mel shuffles her feet, her hands clasping behind her back, but she doesn't say a thing.

"*Puuunkin?*" Hunter prods and finally, the girl speaks.

"Fine. She called me a little while ago, said she just wanted us to know that she was okay and for us not to worry. That she just needed to do some stuff on her own and she couldn't be around that buffoon anymore." She steps into the office, coming as close to me as Hunter's body between us will allow. "With how upset she was, I suggest you leave her the hell alone. That girl has had enough trauma to last her a lifetime, and she sure as fuck doesn't need any from you."

Hearing that Hayley is upset puts a lead ball in my stomach. The thought of her out there all alone, crying. I can't bear it.

"Wait, you said she called. Her cell phone. We can trace it."

Jace sighs, holding up a mobile device. "You mean this

one? She left it behind. And based on the footage from the gas station, she used a pay phone."

"A pay phone? They still have those?" Jack huffs while rubbing at his scruff.

"I'm fucked. All we have is that she's gone North." I stumble backward until my ass is hitting the leather sofa. "What am I gonna do? Hayley's out there. Upset because of me, and there's nothing I can do to bring her back."

"Stop that negative shit right now." Austin comes up behind me and smacks me upside the head. "We're going to find her. And when we do, you're going to apologize for whatever it is you did wrong, including thinking she was the mole. Hell, if I can forgive Hunter for his major secret, then she'll be able to forgive you. That girl had nothing but hearts in her eyes whenever she looked at you."

"*Hold up.* You thought Hayley was the mole?!" Mel screeches and I wince.

The more I think about it, the more ridiculous it sounds. But I don't even bother disputing it at this point. I'm an asshole to think the worst of my angel and I deserve any wayward comment or look her best friend throws my way.

Right now, I just pray that we find her. And I swear that when I do, I'll spend the rest of my life making it up to her.

HAYLEY

My mind is a blur as I step into the assisted living facility. It's been about six months since I was here last, but the scent of disinfectant is just as I recall.

Everything is a pale shade of grey, and the stench of decay is heavy despite how cold and sterile it is. *Ugh.* I hate that this is where Mother will have her last breath.

The thought of that has my stomach churning and I wish now more than ever that father would relinquish his guardianship over her. *But he won't.* Now that I've messed up his chance of getting the Tortured Crown shares, that's never going to happen.

I didn't tell Mel the whole truth. It wasn't just weekends off that Father bargained. He'd also swore that he'd let me take over Mother's care.

"Ms. Barclay, so nice to see you," the nurse behind the counter greets me. "Your mother is doing well today."

I don't even bother asking if that means her memory has returned. I lost hope of that ever happening on year three.

From what the doctors said, her traumatic brain injury caused serious impairment of not only cognitive function, but extensive memory loss. Mother requires around the clock care, something Father deemed a burden and, of course, it's something else I owed him for.

"Had it not been for your selfish actions, your mother would've never been hit by that car! So from now on, every paycheck you make goes to keeping your mother here."

Father's words as we dropped Mother off replay in my head and the real reason of why I started working for my father at sixteen unveils. It wasn't because he thought me a marketing prodigy or because he wanted to instill in me an amazing work ethic. *No.* It was to repay my sins.

"There you are, pretty girl." Mother's cheery tone has me breaking out of my self-pity. "Did you put the chickens up?"

Every time I see her. Every. Damn. Time.

"Yes, sissy. I sure did." I repeat like all the others, knowing she's mistaken me for her sister.

Mother grew up on a farm in West Texas with her sister and both parents. Apparently, the brain injury caused her to regress and now every time I see her, she thinks I'm her sister.

Unfortunately, I never met Aunt Sally. She was in the car that got mowed over by a drunk driver. Mother lost her parents and sister all in one night.

"Good. I hate barn chores. But you already know that." She grabs my hand and pulls me to the bed. "But something I don't hate is that cute ranch hand."

Mother swoons and I stifle a giggle. I have no clue who this ranch hand was or where he is today, but mother loves to go on and on about him, so I let her. It's a welcomed distraction from what's really going on in my life.

"Father always makes fun of his accent, but I think it's *so* exotic." She fans herself as her cheeks flush. "You know, everyone thinks he won't ever amount to much. But when we're alone, he speaks of his dreams, and I believe them. I believe in him. I know that one day, he'll be *El Jefe*."

My brows push together at that name. She's said it countless times before, so why does this sense of *déjà vu* feel different?

"*El Jefe?*" I repeat.

"Yes. It's so hot the way he says it. I can feel the fire in his eyes, and the conviction in his soul." Mother abruptly rises from the bed. "Oh, I'm all hot and bothered now. I need to go splash my face." She shoots me a grin before disappearing into the attached bath.

Weird. I can't shake this feeling. As if I were missing some piece to the puzzle.

Footsteps in the hall have my eyes drifting to the threshold when the last person I expected to see walks through.

"Radley? What are you doing here?"

He laughs. "As if the boss man would let you go a day without him." He's rolling his eyes, but the mention of Matthew has my chest squeezing.

"How'd he find me?" I left my phone behind on purpose. With all the security they have on staff, I wasn't chancing him tracing my location.

"It was luck, really. Has a search party going in all directions. I just happen to be one of the men who traveled north. Kept an ABP out for the stolen car, and here we are." He tsks as he gets closer. "You know, Sara isn't too happy about that."

My heart beats faster with every step he takes. He

might be here for Matthew, but I still don't trust him to keep his slimy hands to himself.

"Yeah, well, I couldn't take a chance on her rejecting my request." I shrug my shoulders as I get up from the bed, needing to create more space between us.

Just then, the bathroom door opens and Mother steps out. "Oh, I swear. Every time I think about that boy my whole body can't help but react." She's laughing as she walks toward me, only to stop cold upon noticing Radley in the room.

"I'm sorry, sissy. I didn't know you had company. Should I..." She points her thumbs toward the bathroom, and I'm not sure how to handle this situation.

I can't very well tell her I'm not sissy, that this is not a booty call, and that I've technically run away from a lockdown.

Radley's been giving her his back this entire time, but just then he turns and the look on my mother's face is one of adoration. *What the fuck?*

"Ramon? Is that you? Did you come for me?" Her look of adoration quickly turns to hurt, and not a moment later, terror fills her eyes. "Hayley, get away from him!"

Hayley? Did she just say my name?

"Now, Miranda, is that any way to talk to your lover?" Radley walks to the door before quietly shutting it behind him. "What will our daughter think of me with you acting like a battered woman?"

Mother quickly steps between us, her arms going out

protectively. "I don't know what you think you're doing here, Ramon. We had a deal. I would raise her as my own and you would go on, living the life of your dreams and aspirations with your chosen wife and multiple whores."

My mind is a blur. None of this makes sense. "I'm sorry. Is *he* the ranch hand?"

Radley...*err*... Ramon Chuckles. "That was many lifetimes ago. I married into Cartel royalty, became *El Jefe*, and along the way had my share of indiscretions."

Mother scoffs. "I should have known that's all I was to you. An indiscretion."

There's anger in her tone, but I detect the hurt too.

"No, *mi amor*. You were my one true love. The one I could never have. Not because I didn't want to, but because there is nothing good about me, and keeping you both would've only tarnished you with my filth."

I feel Mother shake, her next words coming out rocky. "That wasn't your decision to make. You took that from me!"

Ramon sighs. "There's no denying life would have been so different if I'd given you that choice. But what's done is done." He takes a few steps forward and pulls Mother's hand to his. "I'm sorry, my love. For the longest time I thought I'd lost you because of that wretched car accident. But maybe this is our second chance, and now that you have your memory back, maybe this is when we can rebuild what we've lost."

She can't be buying this horseshit, right?

"Ramon, I don't know. I just…this just… it's all so fast. I feel like I'm missing this huge block of time. Everything's so fuzzy now. I need more time." There she is, my practical mother. The woman who taught me how to take things slow and always be cautious.

Ramon slowly nods, both of his hands clapping over my mothers. "You're right, *mi amor*. Let me get a doctor so he can go over your chart. At the very least, maybe we can get you out of this horrid facility and into my home. I bet you'd make rapid recovery under my care."

He finally releases his hold on her and walks toward the door, looking over his shoulder one last time before stepping over the threshold.

Mother is positively beaming as I whirl her around to face me, and I fear we don't have much time. "Mom, something doesn't feel right. I know you just got your memory back, but you have to trust me. I've known Radley, and the new version of him is anything but kind and generous. Something's off and we can't stay here waiting to figure it out."

"Radley? Who's Radley?" Mom's brows furrow and she looks so lost and confused.

I feel guilty putting all of this on her when she should be recovering. I'd hate to hinder her progress with all this new information.

"I'm sorry. I meant Ramon. Ramon has been going as Radley for the past year or so. At the very least. He's been working for Matthew Crown, but if he has ties to the cartel like he admitted, then there's more to this than meets the eye. We have to get away. At least until we've got this all sorted and we know who we can trust."

Mother is nodding, her face serious. "Okay. But how?"

My head flings to the window. It's the only way. I'm just thankful we're on the first floor.

Seems like she's tracked my thinking because Mother beats me to it, her feet carrying her directly to the nearest exit.

"Do you have a car?" she asks while opening the glass pane.

"Yup. It'll take us far enough away to regroup." My feet are landing on the dirt outside when I hear the door open and Radley curse. "*Go!*" I hiss, grabbing hold of her hand before pulling us toward the parking lot.

"*Get back here!*" Radley screams behind us as we finally reach the pavement, but I know we won't make it to the car in time. I'm parked clear across the lot, near the entrance.

But as if an answer to a prayer, I see him. Spencer, the sheriff. Oh, thank God!

Radley wasn't lying about the APB. Never have I been gladder to have stolen a car. At least it led the sheriff straight to me.

"Spencer! Spencer, over here!" I'm yanking mother toward the squad car when he turns, spotting us both.

"Hayley? What's going on? What's wrong?" Concern mars his features and instantly I feel safer.

Slowing down only as I reach him, I speak as fast as I'm able. "Radley, he's not really who he says he is." I turn to see him closing the distance between us and know I don't have much time. "You need to get us out of here, he's dangerous."

"I agree." Spencer looks behind me and nods. "Get in the car. I'll handle this."

He opens the rear door and motions for us to get in.

"But you shouldn't—" I go to speak but Spencer shakes his head.

"Get in the car, Hayley. He won't hurt me." He raises an expectant brow, and I at least know the inside of the car is safe. It's got bullet proof windows, right?

I go in first and Mother follows with Spencer shutting the door behind her. It's not until I'm fully seated that I let out the breath I was holding. Although we aren't totally in the clear, I know that Spencer will at least bring me back to Matthew, and he's definitely the lesser of the two evils.

Chapter Twenty-Five
HAYLEY

"Are you sure we shouldn't just go back inside?" Mother worries her bottom lip and I feel horrible for putting her through this.

It's like she's been asleep this entire time, only to wake up in a living nightmare.

"I think this might be best for now." My eyes drift outside to where Spencer has met Ramon in the field between the building and the parking lot.

It looks like a heated exchange, and I just pray that my biological father doesn't have a gun on him. *This is so surreal.* Bile crawls up my throat at the memory of our first encounter in the elevator. Did he know I was his daughter then?

"If you think so, buttercup." Mother's term of endearment breaks me out of my thoughts and makes my heart stutter.

It's been ages since I've heard it and knowing that I might have a chance at a normal relationship with her again has my heart reeling.

"Do you remember what happened? What got you here?" My heart pumps as I wait for an answer.

I don't deserve this. I don't deserve her.

"It's all a bit foggy, but I remember fighting with Parker..." her eyes go glassy as she looks past me. "Oh, God! Hayley, I'm so so sorry! I never meant for you to find out that way."

She's grabbing my shoulders, shaking me before bringing me in for a firm embrace.

"No, I'm the one who's sorry." I cry, unable to hold back the floodgate of guilt I've carried for so long. "It's all my fault. This is all my fault."

My chest twists, and the lump in my throat is too hard to swallow.

"Shhh. Buttercup, it's okay. You were just a child. I was your momma doing what momma bears do." She presses a soothing hand to the back of my head, her soft strokes comforting even though I know I don't deserve them.

Snot bubbles from my nose, and the tears keep dripping

down my face. "But I should've known better. I knew you were chasing me. If I hadn't run out into the street…"

Mother pushes me far enough back so that our eyes meet. "Now you listen to me, and you listen to me good. You *are* my daughter. And as your mother, I'd follow you into the pits of Hell if I had to, just to keep you safe."

I choked sob rips from my chest. *This*. It's pure unconditional love. *A mother's love.*

My arms wrap around my stomach defensively and I know that's exactly what I'd give Matthew's baby. I feel my face scrunch as my thoughts drift back to the last time we were together. He *wanted* me to take his seed. He *wanted* me to have his child.

But why if it was all a lie? Why, if he was only trying to trick me?

I'm not given much time to ponder because shots ring out and I instinctively crouch, bringing Mother with me. "Stay down."

"Oh god, do you think they're okay?" Mother goes to look out the window, but I drag her back down.

"No! I just got you back. I will not have you shot!"

"Do you think Ramon's been hit?" Her face heats and I know a part of her still thinks he's good. "He may look and act differently than when I saw him last, but his eyes, they're still the same. I couldn't bear the thought of them dimming."

Yup. She still thinks there's a good man hiding in there somewhere. But can I really blame her? Love makes us blind. Just look at Matthew and me. *Ugh.* I get it, but I don't like it.

It's quiet now, neither the men arguing or guns going off fill the air. "Maybe it's safe to look now?"

I sit up straight just as the driver's door opens and Spencer gets in.

"Ladies, you were right to run from that psychopath."

Mother's breath stutters as she sits upright. "Is he okay? Did you shoot him?"

I see Spencer's brows furrow through the rearview mirror. "No ma'am. It was just a few warning shots, but he got the message."

"So, are we going back to the ranch?" My eyes narrow as I peer outside, the hairs on the back of my neck standing on edge. Something still doesn't feel right. *Something's missing.*

Spencer grunts, his head bobbing in confirmation. "It's a bit of a drive, but we'll get there soon enough."

He starts the engine as the thoughts in my head settle. It's been a wild day, but the past hour has definitely taken the cake. It's upturned the last five years of my life. *Radley is Ramon. Ramon was my mother's lover, and they are both my true biological parents.* These new revelations have left me with a million questions. I don't even know where to start.

"What's wrong?" Mother squeezes my hand, her eyes focused intently on my face.

"You're really my mom?" I feel the pressure build

behind my lids and know tears will soon follow. "All this time, I thought I was this dirty secret…" I laugh, but it's full of sadness. "I guess I still am, what with my father being—"

I look toward Spencer, and even though he's the sheriff, I don't want to divulge information Matthew might use as leverage. Thankfully, Mother catches my drift, her eyes shifting back and forth between our driver and me.

"We'll talk later, darling. First, let's catch our breath." She pats my hand as her eyes drift to the countryside passing by. It's late evening, and the sky is painted in the prettiest shades of pink and orange. It's breathtaking, and a welcomed reprieve from the ugly we've had to endure.

I'll take it. Leaning back, I look out the window and let the scenery soothe my tired soul.

The adrenaline that'd been coursing through me starts to dissipate and I feel my body wanting to crash as fatigue settles over me. *Sleep.* Maybe that'll help me face what's up ahead. I let my eyes flutter closed while Mother holds my hand.

A nap. Just a short one to help sort out my head.

I know Matthew isn't much safer than Ramon, at least not for my heart, but maybe now that we know the truth about *El Jefe* being under his nose, he'll have what he needs. Taking that information to the feds should clear his family's name, right?

Matthew

"The men of WRATH have eyes on Sara's vehicle. It was abandoned at an assisted living facility north of here."

My brows push together. "Assisted living facility?"

Jack nods. "Footage shows her going in through the main entrance, but never coming out."

My heart races at the implications of his words. "Is she okay? Was she taken?"

My eldest brother steps toward me, both of his hands going to either of my shoulders. "She was visiting her mom. Miranda Barclay. Apparently, she suffered a traumatic brain injury five years ago and had severe memory loss paired with other cognitive issues."

Titus' words flash in my mind's eye. He'd started to tell me about Hayley's mother when all hell broke loose outside the station.

"Right, okay. So she was visiting her mother. That still doesn't explain what happened to her and why she's missing."

Jack's fingers dig into my shoulders, and I know what he's about to say isn't any good.

"Radley was seen entering the building shortly after her arrival." He stares at me, his jaw clenching while he lets me process his words.

"Radley? As in my employee, Radley?" The tip of my tongue dances across the sharp edge of my teeth. "There's no way he would've known where she was unless it was some freak coincident or…"

"He'd been tailing her." Hunter finishes my sentence, the one I'd been hesitant to voice out loud.

"But why?" I'm shaking my head, trying to piece it all together. "Is he obsessed with her? Jesus. I know I'm older than Hayley, and probably don't have room to talk, but that man is actually old enough to be her father."

My stomach revolts as I think back to the way he leered in Hayley's office. His groin was pressed up firm against that desk. If I recall, he might've had a fucking hard-on.

A roar rips from my throat as I push Jack away. "I'm gonna kill him!" I'm pacing like a madman, gripping my hair so tight, I'm bound to rip it out. "Where are they?! Where the fuck are they!?"

"We're working on it, brother. Don't worry. We'll find her." Hunter speaks as he taps away at his phone. "I've been trying to reach Spencer, see if he has any connections up north, but he isn't answering."

"Of course he isn't. That self-serving asshole is only around when it benefits him." I grab my keys and head toward the door.

"Wait! Where are you going?" Jack calls off behind me.

"North, apparently." My stomach knots at my ineptitude. "I should've left as soon as she'd gone missing. My girl needs me, and there's no way I can help her from the Ranch."

"But you still don't know where she is? She could be anywhere right now, and you'd only be getting farther away."

Another roar falls from my lips, my closed fit hitting the wall and breaking through the plaster. "This is *bullshit*!"

"*Oh god.*" Hunter mutters off to my left and the chilling tone in his voice pulls my attention immediately.

"What? Spit it out Hunter." I'm glaring at my brother, urging him to speak or suffer the consequences.

"Security just sent me the parking lot footage…"

I'm not liking where this is going. "And?"

"Looks like Hayley and another woman approached a squad car before getting in the back."

"Squad car. Police. They're safe, right?" My heart is pounding in my ears, because despite that being the logical assumption, my intuition is telling me otherwise.

Hunter sighs, running a palm over his face. "It's Spencer's car."

I blink once with pause. "Spencer. The same Spencer you can't reach?"

My brother nods, his lips forming into a thin line.

"Fuck." Jack hisses behind me. "Would it be out of the realm of possibility to think he's got shit reception?"

"It's a fucking patrol vehicle. He's got SAT on that thing!" I pace furiously back and forth, the keys digging into my palm and piercing the calloused skin. "None of this makes sense. Why were Radley and Spencer both there? I get that Radley might have an obsession with Hayley, but why Spencer? God, does he want her too?"

"Calm down, brother. You're about to burst a vessel." Jace tries to hand me a drink, but I don't want it. I don't want to numb this pain away. I deserve to feel every excruciating second. This is all my fault. I'm the reason she ran. I'm the reason she's upset. And now I'm the reason she's gone missing.

"Hey, at least now we know what we're looking for. It'll be easier for the men of WRATH to track them down." Hunter tries to give me the silver lining to this revelation, but I am in no mood to celebrate any wins.

Nothing is a victory until I've got Hayley in my arms.

Chapter Twenty-Six
HAYLEY

"Hayley, wake up." Mother shakes me from my restless nap.

"Mom?" I squint as my body jostles in the seat. Looking out the window, it's pitch black, but it's obvious we're on an old dirt road.

"Is this where the ranch is?" Mother whispers as Spencer continues to drive us deeper into the woods, the headlights shining the path forward through a thicket of trees.

No. This is definitely not the way to the ranch.

"Uh, Spencer? Where are we going?" My voice cracks,

either from sleep or the eerie suspicion that things have taken a dark turn. "Spence?"

Nothing. He doesn't speak a word.

I know there's plexiglass between us, but surely he can hear me. *Yes, he definitely can.* My thoughts go back to when he first entered the car. He heard us then so he can hear me now.

Fear has my blood running cold and my heart picking up its pace. "Spencer! Answer me!" I pound on the barrier, demanding he respond. "I won't stop screaming until you do!"

I keep going, pounding, and calling his name. *Wherever he's taking me, I'm not going without a fight.*

"Enough!" Finally, our captor answers. "You'll see soon enough."

Just as his last word falls from his lips, we hit a clearing and a small cabin comes into view.

"I take it this isn't the ranch?" Mother's question makes the sheriff chortle.

"Well, aren't you bright?"

"Hey, don't talk to her like that!" I give the glass one more punch, daring him to do it again.

Gone is the timid Hayley, cowing down to every threat. No, the new me won't stand for this bullshit, and I sure as hell am not letting him take us into that creepy as fuck cabin. At least not before clawing his skin off.

"I'm not sure you're in any position to make demands, *little doll.*" Spencer's use of that term makes my stomach roil. It's Matthew's, and hearing it come out of the sheriff's mouth just sounds so wrong.

"You can't stop me from demanding anything. Now, whether you do it, that's on your conscience. You still have time to make things right, you know? Take us to Matthew and I'll give you information on *El Jefe*." It's the only thing I have to barter. The knowledge that the man the feds have been after is still alive and has been under their nose this entire time.

"You stupid girl. You think I'm not aware of that? That *El Jefe* is alive?"

And as if I needed more proof of my assumptions, Ramon steps in front of the car, the headlights showcasing his wicked grin.

"What do you want, Ramon!?" Mother screams, capturing our attention. "I told you I would stay out of your way, keep all your dirty secrets. All that I asked of you was for you to leave my daughter alone!"

"Our daughter, Miranda. And that agreement went out the window when the Crown family stole from me. They have all my wealth—everything I worked so hard for—hidden amongst them, and I intend to get it back. Even if it means sacrificing my daughter's life."

Great. Just fucking great. I have Matthew willing to torture me, my bio dad willing to kill me, and my non-bio dad willing to whore me out for shares.

If ever I needed more confirmation that it was high-time I stood up for myself, this is it. I am my own hero. I am my own first responder.

And as Spencer opens the door to pull me out, I do the first thing I can think of—I punch him in the nuts and run.

"Run, Mother! Run!" I shout, moving my feet as fast as I can muster.

I hear a yelp and my heart squeezes. I know it. They've got her.

"Run and she dies." Spencer's holding Mother up by her hair, her thin frame cowering below him.

"Save yourself, Hayley. Keep going!" Mother's voice cracks as a slap rings in the air and I know they've hit her.

I can't run.

All this time, I harbored guilt over what happened to her. I will not fail her again.

Hiding behind a tree, I shout out my last demand. "A life for a life. I'll come back to you willingly if you let her go."

Spencer cackles. "And why would we do that?"

"Because the Crown men don't have a stake in her, but they do me. They'd give you back your assets in exchange for my life. But they might not for just hers."

"Hayley, don't do that! Go, baby! Go!" Mother pleads, but it's falling on deaf ears. There's no way I'm leaving her behind.

"So, what's it gonna be?" I prod, knowing that I'm just bluffing. They *have* to take my offer.

A pause ensues and all I hear is my own breathing, anxiety ratcheting up with every second that goes by.

I'm on the verge of a panic attack when Ramon finally answers. "Deal."

Letting out a sigh of relief, I step from behind the large Spruce. "Okay, release her on the count of three. We'll both walk toward the middle." I'm banking on the fact that they'll want me alive in order to barter their deal. But I'm not too sure they'd do the same for her. "And no shooting at Mother!"

Neither reply, but Spencer starts the count. "One, two, three—"

I see them release her and start on my path toward the cabin. I don't know what awaits me, but it can't be anything good. Either way, as I reach Mother, I know I've made the right choice.

She quickly pulls me in for a hug and I feel her whole body tremble. "I can't leave you here, buttercup. I won't."

I squeeze her tight before whispering in her ear. "You have to. I can buy us time until you find help."

"Enough with the hugging! Either release her or we'll shoot you both." Spencer snarls and I quickly do as he says.

She's our only hope of getting help, and I will not risk it for an extended hug.

Begrudgingly, Mother nods, her jaw clenching and eyes glazing over before she turns and runs into the woods.

"*Goodbye*," I whisper into the dark, praying that I find a way back to her, back to the life I once had.

Matthew

"We're almost there. Hang on, brother." Jack urges me to stay calm when I feel anything but.

I'm ready to tear my hair out, needing to get eyes on my girl right-the-fuck-now.

Not soon enough, the SUV comes to a stop. Where in a thicket of trees somewhere in Brown's Park. Based on what Hayley's mother has told us, Spencer and Radley are in cahoots, and I still can't wrap my head around it.

"Damn, you got here quick." Titus raises a brow as we approach their makeshift camp. That's when I see her, a fragile woman wrapped in a blanket as she clutches a mug of something steaming.

"Well, I would've gotten here quicker, but y'all have the chopper down in Florida."

Jack snorts. "Uh, we're supposed to have the element of surprise. I highly doubt that'd be possible if we flew a helicopter in."

"Brother, I'm ready to go in guns blazing if necessary."

"I know you are," Titus claps a hand on my shoulder. "And that's why we're here. To prevent you from doing anything stupid that could cost you your girl's life."

My blood boils, knowing it was one of their men that let her slip through the gate in the first place. But now is not the time to point fingers. There'll be time for dishing out hell later, but first we need to get Hayley back.

I nod toward the woman. "That her mom?"

Titus nods. "Yeah, she stumbled across a young couple who'd been camping in the park. Thank God they had SAT phones. We'd set up perimeters given their last known location and intercepted the call with the help of local law enforcement."

My brows raise. "That's a surprise, given that Spencer is one of them. I'd think they'd want to cover for him."

"Nah," Titus shakes his head. "Turns out he's been dirty, and they all knew it. He's been causing problems for a while now."

Wow. How in the fuck did we not see it?

"So, what now?" I raise a brow, waiting to hear their plan, and it better be good. "Because believe me, I'm willing to go in there, guns blazing."

"No! *El Jefe*, he'll kill her." Hayley's mother abruptly stands, the blanket and mug falling away.

"*El Jefe*?" All the men say in unison.

A chill runs up my spine and I just know this fucked up situation is about to get worse.

"Yes. Ramon." Her brows are furrowed as she looks between us, and I wonder if she's delusional. Didn't one of my brothers say she had cognitive issues?

"Ma'am." I step closer to her, taking my time so as not to scare her. "There are only two people holding Hayley captive. Radley and the sheriff, Spencer Brown."

She shakes her head, her brows dropping even further. "No, no. My Hayley, she'd said he was going by a new name now. But that Radley, he's Ramon. He's *El Jefe*."

Okay, clearly this lady is off her rocker and I'm beginning to wonder if Hayley is even in that cabin.

"That can't be, ma'am. *El Jefe* is dead. His brother killed him. Murdered him in cold blood."

"I'm telling you, that's him. I know the father of my child." She wrings her hands, her eyes manic. "He threatened to kill Hayley, not caring that she's his daughter. He'll do it, too. I know it."

My body goes numb and all I hear is a ringing in my ear. *El Jefe is alive, and he's Hayley's father?* I'm in a daze as I process everything she's just said.

"But how?" I turn to Titus who's already on the phone, his finger in the air urging me to hold. "I thought you said Raul murdered *El Jefe*?"

He says something in Spanish before turning to face me once more. "I'm on the phone with the Cardenas family. *El Jefe* and Raul were in their custody when this happened."

"Tell my father-in-law I say hi." Jack mutters under his breath while rubbing at his temples. I'm sure he's not thrilled, what with him poised to take over upon el Don's retirement. But a deal's a deal, and that was the only way that man would let Penelope marry Jack. *Well, the only way without bloodshed.*

"*Okay, esta bien. Si. Entiendo.*" Titus makes a disgruntled sound before he's speaking into the receiver. "*No. Sigue vivo.*"

"What the fuck is going on?" God, how I wish I remembered something, anything, from my high school Spanish.

Finally, Titus cuts the line but the look in his eyes is far from comforting.

"Cardenas' men were under attack at the time, and the man they saw being murdered *could've* been a stand-in. A sacrifice to get everyone off *El Jefe's* tail. It isn't uncommon for prominent leaders to have someone stand in the limelight, while they hide in the shadows and take care of business."

"Could've been a stand-in?" I whisper. "Could've been a fuckin' stand-in?!" I roar. "This is unacceptable! All this time we were operating under the assumption that *El Jefe* was dead. All of this time we'd been looking for his accomplices when the very man who started this war was right under our noses!"

Right under your nose. "That slippery mother fucker! Spencer was in on it all along. He's probably the fucking mole!"

Jack growls. "Of course he's the mole."

Rage rips through me, my blood burning hot. "Yeah, he's a fucking rodent. And it's time we *exterminate*."

Chapter Twenty-Seven
MATTHEW

"*Now*. We move out together, or I go in alone. I'm done waiting." I double check my gear, making sure I have enough ammo and that my comms are all on.

The men of WRATH have been running recon, and it feels like an eternity since their last perimeter check.

"Brother, just wait until we've received the go ahead from security. They—"

A loud blood-curdling scream sounds off in the woods and the only thing not sending me into a blind rage is the fact that it was clearly male.

"What the fuck?" Jack looks into the inky night as I

head toward the sound. "Matthew, wait!"

"No. I'm done waiting. Clearly, some shit is going down and I will not sit here with a thumb up my ass while my girl is in obvious peril."

The trudging of boots behind me lets me know that the men are following suit. *Good.* I'd still go it alone, but it's nice to know I have backup.

And this becomes especially true after trekking into a gruesome site. "*Wow.* To think that this was less than a mile from camp."

We've stumbled upon two decaying bodies way past rigor mortis. Their flesh has taken on a green tinge and the bodies are bloated as they fill with gas.

"Is that? Are those?" Jack asks as he stares in horror. "You don't think it was the campers, do you? We left Miranda back there."

"Nah. This is closer to the cabin. My money is on the known sociopaths as opposed to the lovebirds." Austin's nose wrinkles and his mouth turns down. "Either way, we should message base and let them know."

I nod in agreement. "Yeah. This is definitely cartel related. Heads are severed and whoever did it couldn't even be bothered to hide the evidence. It's either the work of a narcissist or *El Jefe* and his men. My money's on the latter"

"I don't think it was *El Jefe*," Titus speaks through my earpiece. He must've deviated from the path at some point because he's nowhere to be seen.

I speak into the mic, demanding an answer. "Where are you?"

"Down the trail."

How in the fuck did he move past us? No matter. He's closer to the cabin than we are and I'm eager as hell to get this show on the road. "Let's move."

I lead us down the path that's nothing more than a deer trail, and soon enough we spot Titus and his creepy-as-fuck grin.

"What's got you smiling like that?" I raise a brow, skeptic as hell.

"It's Radley." His lips roll in and he's trying to hold back a laugh.

What in the actual—Holy shit! I'm standing next to Titus, peering into the outhouse floor. But it's gone, and in its place is a deep hole, complete with spikes and the impaled body of one slimy ass motherfucker.

"Holy shit is right. I guess I won't be having that heart-to-heart with dear ol' dad after all." Austin peers into the hole before turning back toward me.

"I'm sorry?" It comes out a question because I'm not sure how to respond. Would I want to talk to my father knowing he was the sociopath who caused my family pain? "Shit. You probably wanted to do the honors yourself."

"What's done is done. At least the way he went out wasn't pretty." Austin shrugs, his eyes devoid of emotion as he goes back to staring at the gore below. "So I take it this is Spencer's handy work, then?"

"Looks like it," I sneer. "And now that psychopath is all alone with my girl."

Not wasting another second, I turn and head back down the trail. Time is of the essence, and every tick of the clock is a moment too long.

Hayley

Fifteen minutes earlier

"I'm still pissed at you." Spencer glowers at Ramon as he stokes the fire in the small cabin.

Everything in here is right out of some slasher movie. From the furniture that hasn't been touched in ages, all covered in a thick layer of dust, to the boarded-up windows with rotting wood. *And the smell.* It's a mixture of damp and decay.

Even the chair I'm in feels brittle, as if it were to break at any given moment. Now, if i could just free myself from these bindings…

"What? This place is hundreds and hundreds of acres. Heavily wooded. There's no way she'll find a way out." Ramon shrugs his shoulders callously. "She won't survive. Not trekking out there all alone in nothing but a thin dress and some slippers. The way I see it, Mother Nature will spare us the trouble and finish her off instead."

"You're heartless," I hiss. "She loved you. How could you talk about her like that?!"

Ramon cackles. "My dear child, love is for fools." He walks toward me, eyes blazing with nothing but evil. "The minute you give your heart away to someone is the moment you've lost. They will take it and destroy it, without a care in the world."

"If you two are done with your daddy-daughter bonding, can we get back to what's important? *The land, the money, the gold.*"

Ramon sighs before turning back toward Spencer. "*Ugh.* You're insufferable."

"Yeah, yeah. That's nothing new." He stands from his crouched position before crossing his arms in front of his chest. "So are we calling in the ransom, or what?"

"Not until Raul and Catherine get here." My biological father sighs once more as he walks to the door. "I need to make sure they're both safe. Those fucking men of WRATH have obliterated my men and I can't afford to lose one more."

Spencer snorts. "As if those two would do you any good."

"Watch your tongue, or you'll end up without it. That's my brother and daughter you're talking about."

Pain hits me square in the chest. How could I be jealous of a sister I never met? Still, the fact that he cares more about her safety than mine… it stings.

"Fine, old man. We'll wait for them." Spencer sighs.

"Good. I'm glad you understand." Ramon walks to the

door. "We can talk about the logistics of the ransom later. Right now, I need to take a piss."

"I swear you have the bladder of a goldfish." Spencer grunts. "You remember where the bathroom is, right?"

"I sure as fuck do, *pendejo*." Ramon pushes on the door to the outside and groans. "You couldn't pick a place with indoor plumbing?"

"Come on. The outhouse isn't *that* bad." Spencer smirks, and I have a feeling it really is that bad.

"It's disgusting. I used it the last time we were here, and I swear I've smelt decaying bodies that had a more pleasant odor."

"See!? Bladder of a goldfish! Always using the bathroom." Spencer laughs while Ramon flips him the finger.

"Go fuck yourself." Ramon spits out before closing the door behind him.

Shit. Now it's just Spencer and me, this realization blanketing me in a sea of uneasiness. And as my lone captor turns to face me, I know that my intuition is spot on.

"Finally. Alone at last," Spencer whispers, his words sending an icy chill running through me.

The broad man turns, and although he isn't as tall as Matthew, he's easily over six feet in height.

"I don't like the way you're looking at me, Spencer." I press myself against the chair, the rope digging into my wrists where they meet.

"What? I just want to see what the fuss is all about." He's looming over me, letting his calloused fingers trace the outline of my face. "All of you women. You turn these Crown men into savages, willing to put their own lives on the line just to keep you safe."

My stomach revolts, the bile burning on its way up. "That's right, they will seek and destroy anything that threatens to harm us. Matthew is no different. He will find you, and he will make you pay."

I'm full of shit. I'm not a Crown woman. I know the truth. Matthew was willing to turn me over in exchange for his family's safety. But that doesn't stop me from pretending. In part, to give this man pause and the other, because maybe I wish it were true.

Especially now, as Spencer takes out a knife and presses it against my jugular.

"Little doll, he's gonna have a hard time finding you. I've already disposed of Catherine and Raul." He looks toward the door and snickers. "And soon, *El Jefe* will be gone too."

"What are you talking about? That man is more of a psychopath than you are. Anyone willing to off their own flesh and blood is. If he comes in here and catches you playing with his bait, he's gonna be pissed."

"Stupid girl. You think I'd be willing to risk the loot I've worked so hard for? I've put in years with that man. And for what? To split my winnings with his bastard child and brother? Fuck no. For that matter, *El Jefe* can suck it right along with them." He digs the knife a little deeper. "That outhouse is rigged. And as soon as he steps inside, he's plunging to his untimely death. So, you better do what I say, or this blade'll slit right along that pretty throat." Spencer's mouth splits into a lecherous grin, the rough pad of his thumb forcefully swiping at my lips. "This mouth, I bet it'd look real pretty wrapped around my cock."

I whimper just as a loud cracking sounds off to my left and we turn just in time to see the cabin door fly open. Several men pour into the small space, but my eyes are trained on one. *Matthew*. His face is red and the bulging vein in his neck prominent. *Oh, he's pissed.*

"Can't suck what you don't have. And trust me, you'll be missing that appendage real fuckin' soon." The Greek god steps further into the room, his rifle trained on my captor.

He's here. He's really here.

My eyes swell with tears as hysterical laughter falls from my lips. I can't help it. The fear in Spencer's eyes paired with the fruition of what I'd said, that Matthew would come for me and Spencer would pay. *I was so full of shit.* Yet here he is.

"Yeah? You take one more step and your girl gets a brand new necklace." Spencer glares, pressing the blade deeper into my flesh. The tip pierces the delicate skin and I feel the moment he's drawn blood.

"*Stop!*" Matthew roars as warmth trickles down my throat.

As if in suspended animation, the other men freeze, stopping all movement as they wait for direction.

Seconds pass, but no one speaks—Matthew's eyes have gone feral and I'm not sure any sanity remains.

Taking the lead, a man I'd seen at the station finally speaks up. "Spencer, I'm giving you the option of life. You keep that knife pressed to her throat and I can't guarantee that any longer. You know how these Crown men are. He won't stop until he's painting the wall with your blood."

"All I want is what's owed to me. I haven't worked my ass off these past ten years, just to be left in the dust. You took from my boss, and now we're taking it all back." Spencer walks behind me, all the while keeping the knife in the same position. "The solution is easy. You hand over all the property, including the gold bullion, and I'll let her go."

"We?" Matthew cackles. "There is no we. *Radley* is dead, you made sure of that. And based on your admission, you're responsible for the other decaying corpses we found out back." A look of disgust flashes behind his hazel orbs before fury is consuming them once again. "All that remains is your pathetic excuse for a soul."

Spencer snarls, his cheek lowering to press against mine. "Well, this *pathetic excuse of a soul* has the life of your beloved in his hands, so I suggest you adjust your fuckin' tone."

As if to make his point, Spencer turns toward me and licks a line straight up my cheek. *Oh god. I'm gonna hurl.* I'm shuddering when there's a pop and I'm suddenly covered in chunks of warm sticky liquid.

Ohmyfuckinggod. They shot Spencer in the head. *No.* Matthew shot Spencer in the head.

"Baby!" His large frame rushes toward me as he swings his rifle to the side. "Fuck, I'm so sorry! God, I'm so sorry."

He's apologizing over and over again as I sit here in shock, his hands roaming my body for injuries.

"Tell me you're okay. Please tell me he didn't hurt you." He grabs a hold of my face with one hand while wiping it clean with another.

"You have a kerchief?" It's the first thing I say and apparently it's hilarious because Matthew throws his head back and laughs.

"Yes, I have a kerchief. And good thing I do because I need to kiss those lips to know you're real."

My eyes narrow as I recall what he'd told his brothers. *Even if that means torture.*

"No. You aren't going to kiss me. You're going to untie me and set me free." And I don't just mean physically. This man has a hold on me, one I can't afford to have if I'm to take care of myself.

Any man who wishes me harm doesn't love me. I meant it when I said gone are the days where I was a doormat. And as much as it hurts, I'll have to stay true to the new me, the one that doesn't put up with shit.

"Hayley?" His brows push together, but despite his confusion, he unties the rope at my feet. "I'm sorry. I know I've been hot and cold with you. I know I've demanded a truth when I myself kept lies. I know that I pushed you away."

The men have begun to clear out Spencer's body, but my eyes remain on Matthew. I might still be angry with him, but I'd be lying if I said I didn't want to hear him out.

"*Go on...*" I urge.

"The truth is, I don't deserve you. You're the moon on a dark night. The sunshine after the rain. And I'd be a fool to think I could have you after the way I neglected our special bond. But I am a fool. A fool in love." He moves his hands to the ties around my wrist. "And fools do crazy things."

He's raising a brow, and the wicked gleam in his eyes sends a thrill running through me.

I purse my lips but take the bait. *Hey, I'm only human.* "What kind of crazy things?"

He smiles, the dimple in his cheek cresting. "I'll show you."

"Okay, but that doesn't mean I forgive you. I heard what you said about wanting to torture me… about thinking I was the mole."

"Hmm." Matthew removes the rope and rubs at my wrists. "I admit I was wrong. But between you and me, the only torture I'd ever be willing to inflict would be the kind that eventually got you off."

My face flushes, the images of his admission getting me hot. "As sexy as that sounds now, it doesn't change the fact that you still thought I was capable of being the mole."

Matthew raises a brow. "Hey, let's not forget that I

wasn't the only one holding secrets. Could you really blame me for being weary?"

My mouth opens then closes. He's right. I'd be a hypocrite to deny it. And although I never thought him capable of evil, I sure kept enough secrets to give him doubt as to my intent.

"Fine. *But I'm still mad.*" I pout, only to be met with Matthew's raucous laughter.

"Okay, baby. I promise I'll make it up to you." He lifts me from the chair, carrying me bridal style through the threshold. "But first, we need to get you cleaned up and I need to make sure you're really okay. I mean it. You just had someone explode right next to you and the most emotion I've gotten out of you is a pout."

"Defense mechanism." I let out a harsh breath, my chest shaky with all of the anxiety I'd blocked out. "But I'll be fine. Didn't you hear? I'm Hayley 2.0."

"Doll, I'll love and support every version of you. No matter what."

I purse my lips to the side, my brow arching. "Actions speak louder than words, you know."

He gives me a soft smile full of warmth. "Hayley, my only goal in life is to love you." Matthew looks down at me while waggling his brow. "Well, love you and keep that little cunt happy."

It's my turn to laugh, my head falling back as I take in his strength and humor.

We have a long road ahead of us, but I finally have the

confidence in myself to know that I'll be okay—*no matter what*. That knowledge paired with the fact that this man will support me in whatever it is I choose, it only makes that confidence stronger.

And isn't that what I truly want? A partner who'll support me and be my rock when I need it? One who also vows to keep my kitty happy?

Yeah. That's exactly what I want. *My Matthew Crown.*

Chapter Twenty-Eight
MATTHEW

T*rust*. It's something I know we're both going to have to work on.

And as I lower my future bride, I can't help but take in her newfound strength. Seeing her like this, so sure of herself—*God*, does it make my cock hard.

Knowing that she's capable, but that with me, she surrenders all control. *It's a fucking honor*. One I'll never take lightly.

I brush the hair off her forehead, letting the water cleanse away my multitude of sins before watching them swirl down the drain.

She's a warrior, my girl. Unshaken by what's transpired, ready to take on whatever may come.

"Why are you looking at me like that?" Her nose scrunches and brows furrow.

"What? Like a man in love?"

Hayley's face flushes, before she musters a scowl. "I'm still mad at you."

I twirl her around, her back to me as I rinse off her delectable body. "And *I'm* still mad at *you*."

"Hmm. I don't know why." She purses her lips, but the corner of her mouth turns up in a smirk.

Raising both of her arms, I press her palms to the shower wall before running one of my hands back down along the contours of her body, stopping only once I've reached her tight ass.

"You know I should spank this little peach. Leave it red and raw after what you did. You left the compound knowing full-well there was danger lurking outside. Just about gave me a heart attack."

I moan as Hayley presses her ass into my cock, nestling the steely length between her cheeks.

"Poor, Daddy. Worried about his little girl."

Ahhh fuck. Here we go. Playing this game that drives us both mad. But if insanity is the price to pay, then hand me the fuckin' strait jacket.

"That's right." I grip a hand around her waist and squeeze, while the other goes straight for her juicy tit. "You got poor daddy all worked up."

Hayley squeals as I give her pert nipple a little pinch, her body writhing against my own.

"Oh," she breathes, her head lolling back. "I'm sorry, Daddy. I was a very bad girl, not listening when all you were doing was trying to keep me safe."

Hayley moans as my fingers squeeze and pluck at the hard little nipple. *She loves it.* Her body arching with every pull, begging me for more.

"Yes, you were bad. So bad. *A fuckin' brat.*" I give the side of her luscious breast a quick slap and watch the fat tit jiggle.

"Please, Daddy. Let me make it up to you." She whines as I knead her breast, her head thrashing back and forth.

"And how do you plan on doing that, doll?" I quickly spin her around, wrapping an arm around her waist before pressing her to me. I let my free hand travel up the column of her spine, stopping only once I've reached the hair at her nape and dig my fingers in deep. "Tell me. How are you gonna make it better?"

"I don't know, Daddy." Hayley pouts as she slowly drops to her knees, her eyes focused on mine as she tentatively takes my hard length into her hands. "Maybe…" She licks her bottom lip before pressing a kiss to the tip of my raging hard-on. "Maybe I can be your little fuck doll. Your little whore."

Lord help me. I think my heart just stopped.

Just when I thought this girl couldn't get any more perfect, she surprises me once more.

"You'd do that for Daddy?" I let out a ragged breath, my voice pure gravel.

"Yes, please. I want to make you feel good. I want to make you happy." She mewls, one of her hands dropping to rub between her legs.

"Jesus. How'd I get so lucky? To have such a sweet little thing, made just for me." She's rubbing furiously at her clit. It's clear that the thought of her pleasing me is getting her off and I want in on that action. "Stop. Don't touch that pussy unless I say so. Understood?"

My doll nods, a smile slipping through before she's back to pouting.

"Do you want me to play with this instead?" She grips me with both hands once more, working the shaft from root to tip and my eyes go cross. *Fuck, this feels so good.*

"Yes, baby." My balls are drawing up tight as I push forward, the need to be inside her mouth consuming me whole. "Now open up. It's time to choke on Daddy's cock."

And my angel does just that. With both hands wrapped around the base she brings me to heaven.

"Good girl. Now swallow." *Christ.* I swear I see God himself when the tip of my swollen head reaches the confines of her tight throat. Sparks ignite behind my lids and I can't help but buck, the action making Hayley gag. *Oh, lord.* Before I can stop it, a rogue spurt of cum shoots down her throat. "Jesus, you're so damn hot. I'm not sure I'll be able to take much more of this."

I swipe at a tear trailing down her angelic face. So

sweet and innocent in public, but my filthy whore behind doors.

"*Fuuuuuck*," I groan. How foolish was I to think I could ever let her go?

My knees shake as she takes me in, each suck making my balls grow impossibly heavy with the need to permanently mark her.

"Baby, this cum. As much as I want to shoot it straight down that tight throat, it belongs inside that little cunt. You're mine. You belong to Daddy and I won't be happy until everyone knows it." My hand goes to the top of her head, fingers digging into her hair before slowly pulling her off.

"I wasn't done yet," she pouts.

"Yes, you were, doll. I need inside that pink little hole." In one swift move, I've hoisted her to me, wrapping both of her slender legs around my waist. And with both hands on her ass, I slide her up and down my steely shaft. "Do you feel that, baby? Do you feel what you do to Daddy?"

"Yes!" Hayley throws her head back as her feet press against the back of my thighs. "God, yes!"

She's grinding up and down my massive cock, her body jerking every time her clit bumps against the swollen head.

"This is all you, baby. Getting Daddy all worked up." I let one of my hands fall back before issuing a thundering slap to her ass. "Teasing me with that little cunt before running away. Is that what you wanted, Hayley? To run away?"

"No!" She's trembling in my hold, her eyes rolling back, the one word coming out garbled.

I grip her hips and stop her movement. "Say it louder, doll. Or we'll have to stop."

Hayley digs her nails into my back as she furiously fights against my hold. "No! I promise! No!"

I slide her up my abs until the tip of my cock is seated at her slick little hole.

"*Good girl.*" And with one quick thrust, I push in deep, giving us both what we need.

"*Ohmyfuckinggodholyshit!*" Hayley is gasping for air as she adjusts around my girth. "So full," she breathes.

I lay her back against the wall and take in the sight before me. *Perfection.* Pouty lips, full tits, tiny waist, and *holy mother of god*, that puffy little cunt stretched tight around the root of my fat cock.

My hard length flexes inside of her and she whimpers with need. "What? Is my little girl ready for more?"

I take a thumb and swirl at her pearl, loving how her walls squeeze and contract around me. "Mmmmph." She writhes, swirling her hips and chasing release. "More. I want more."

"Only good girls get what they want. Tell me, Haley. Do you promise to be good?"

"Yes!" Her hands are gripping onto my shoulders, her body taught and on the verge of release. "So good!"

With the pads of my fingers pressed against the top of her womb, I softly strum her clit and whisper, "Perfect, because there's no way I'm holding back. I need to own this pussy. Make it mine."

"Do it." Hayley whimpers, her chest heaving in anticipation. "Stop torturing me and take me. Make me yours."

Torture? It's laughable. The thought that I could inflict pain on this girl. No, the only torture I could ever issue would be more pleasure than penance. But I guess it's torture none the less.

Jesus. I'm an asshole. The thought of that makes me grow another inch, urging me to fuck into her even harder. And, *God,* do I love what I see—Hayley's body bouncing on my cock like a little doll, her full tits bobbing and begging for a lick.

"This what you want, baby?" Hayley's back is sliding up and down the tile wall as I dig my fingers into her hips.

"Yes! Yes! Yes!" She chants with every upward thrust. "Yours. I want to be yours."

I roar at her admission, her truth making me feel like the luckiest man on earth. We've been through hell and back, but this girl, this beautiful angel, she still wants to be mine.

"Always, baby. I'll always be yours." And as I feel her body contract around me, her entire frame going tense, I know she'll always be mine too. "Come for me, doll. Show Daddy how much you love him."

"Matthew!" She shouts, her head thrashing as she gushes her release. "I love you. God, how I love you!"

That's it. *I'm done.*

Her declaration paired with her vice grip on my cock—*Yeah, it does me in.* My balls unleash their full load, and I'm shooting rope after sticky rope of hot cum into my girl. There's no way my seed won't take.

I'm claiming this girl in every way possible, and I won't stop until the whole world knows she's mine. *My very own tortured Crown.*

Epilogue
ERICSON

Three months later...

This is fucking bullshit. It's been ninety days since I left town, waiting for the dust to settle, and I'm over it. I don't give a shit if the case isn't closed and all of the loose ends haven't been mended.

The feds can come at me for all I care. I'm done. Done listening to my former best friend turned brother-in-law and his security team.

Mel and Hunter just had their baby and there isn't shit anyone could do or say that'd keep me away. Despite my not being overly thrilled with who my sister chose to marry, I still love and support her. *No matter what.*

So, keeping that energy, I barge into Jack's ranch, bypassing the million-and-one security.

"Sir, you need to check in!" One of the guard shouts behind me as I head toward the kitchen in need of a drink. It's been a long-ass drive from South Texas, and I'm parched.

"I don't need to do shit. My sister just had her baby and I'm here to celebrate. You—" My words falter as I come across Poppy and a man I'd seen a time or two before. He's one of the men of WRATH security, and he's standing a little too close for comfort.

"Back the fuck up," I growl, but he doesn't budge. "I said—Back. The. Fuck. Up."

The towering man slowly turns to face me, recognition dawning as he flexes his lower lids.

"Ericson. Did you need something?" he asks, but the fucker refuses to take a step back and his body is still touching Poppy's.

"Yeah. I need you to step away from the girl." I raise a brow, begging him to argue.

"Ericson. I don't need you to come in here like some deranged knight in shining armor." Poppy comes out from behind her bodyguard. "Armando and I were having a private conversation. You know? Like the one you and my dad had before he died?"

She's staring daggers at me and if looks could kill,

there's no doubt I'd be six feet under. *I don't care.* There's nothing she could do or say that would ever make me regret keeping that secret from her.

It was a dying man's wish and I wasn't going to let him down. *She'll just have to deal with it.*

"Speaking of your father," I step closer, coming toe-to-toe with Armando. "I know he wouldn't like seeing you canoodling with the likes of him."

Poppy gasps, her arms pushing out to shove me. "Ericson!"

"Everything okay in here?" Austin steps into the kitchen, an arched brow assessing.

"Yes, sir. Ericson here was just about to leave." Armando answers, never taking his eyes from mine.

Oh yeah? Well fuck him.

"No. I'm not leaving, and everything isn't okay. Your man was a little too close to Poppy when I came in. And unless groping is part of his job description, then I'd say things are definitely not okay." I'm staring at the guard as my words register. We're stuck in this game of chicken, and I refuse to be the first to look away.

Austin sighs. "Poppy, is this true?"

Seconds pass without an answer, and I wonder if this is where I truly lose her. I've known her since she was a kid, and I'd be lying if I said I didn't care. Either way, it doesn't matter.

I made a promise to her father, and I intend to keep it. *Whether she likes it or not.*

Poppy

All eyes are on me and I'm not sure how to answer. Armando's been my shadow for the past three months, ever since I was accosted at my diner. It feels like betrayal to admit that he had his hands on me when Ericson walked in.

And Ericson. *God.* Is that one complicated can of worms.

Memories of the last night we were alone together resurface and all of the anger and hurt I'd buried away come bubbling up. He lied to me. Kept a truth so bold it cost me precious time with my father.

"No. It isn't true. Ericson is lying." I stare at him, refusing to look away. Payback's a bitch. He can't have his cake and eat it too. *Lie to me then I'll lie about you.*

"Okay, then." Austin sighs and I see him move closer out of my periphery. "Look, I don't want any problems. Especially not today. It's Mel's party and the last thing we want is an upset woman on jacked up hormones."

Mila groans as she enters the kitchen. "*Awe.* So sensitive of you, brother."

Austin chuckles. "Must be that cold-blooded gene that runs in us both."

"Runs in me, too. Don't forget, we all shared the same degenerate father." Hayley joins us, picking up a mini grilled cheese and popping it into her mouth. "Oh my god,

Poppy. You make the best food! You'll have to cater our wedding."

"Did you and Matthew finally pick a date?" My eyes go as round as saucers as I bypass both Armando and Ericson, bee-lining it straight to my friend.

Hayley snorts. "Yeah, as soon as I pop the next Crown baby out. There's no way I'm walking down the aisle looking like a shotgun bride."

"Hey!" Penelope whines. "There's absolutely nothing wrong with that."

I giggle, knowing Pen was practically full term when she tied the knot with Jack.

"My bad," Hayley mumbles before picking up the tomato soup shooter. "But we better get these to the party tent, or I'm bound to eat them all. This baby has me starving 24/7!"

I chuckle. "Don't worry, there's plenty more where that came from."

"Yeah." Armando, who's normally stoic, speaks up. "She's been up all night, cooking enough for a small army."

Ericson growls. "And were *you* up all night? *With her?*"

Armando scoffs. "Of course, I was. I'm in charge of keeping her safe." He steps toward my father's old friend, refusing to back away from Ericson's hostility. "And that includes keeping her safe from entitled pricks."

"Hey." Austin's firm tone cuts into the moment. "I meant it. I don't want trouble out of you two. Ericson, I don't want to keep you away from your sister, and

Armando, I don't want to send you back to Florida. So, how about we agree to be cordial? At least for today."

There's a beat of silence but both men eventually nod in agreement.

"Good." Austin picks up a platter of sliders. "Men, pick up a tray. We've got some hungry women to feed."

I follow suit, picking up the bite-sized treats and following Mila out the door. Despite both men agreeing to keep it copacetic, I can't help but sense the ominous cloud that lurks above us.

Truth be told, things have been pretty quiet since Parker was sent to the slammer. It was the last 'dramatic' event in three whole months and if feels like something else is about to drop.

Life is never this good for long.

"You okay, Poppy?" Armando's free hand goes to my lower back and I suck in a sharp breath, my eyes turning to find his dark and full of concern.

I'm about to answer when all of a sudden my guard's body goes flying forward, the tray of food going right along with him.

"What the fuck?!" I shriek as Ericson's body pounces on Armando.

"I told you!" He lays into the guard. "Hands off, motherfucker!"

"Fuck you!" Armando is no wilting flower. He maneuvers from underneath, flipping Ericson onto his back. "Poppy isn't your concern."

My guard is about to punch my father's old friend in the face, and I can't bear it. I drop the tray in my hands and jump onto Armando's back. "No! Don't!"

This has both men freezing, as if they were in suspended animation.

"About time we had something exciting happen around here." Mel walks toward us, her adorable baby in hand. "I'm just glad it has nothing to do with me for once."

"Or me!" Hayley giggles as she steps over the bite-sized food scattered all over the floor.

"Ditto." Miranda, Hayley's mother, starts to pickup the *petit fours* I'd dropped before piling them onto the tray.

Everyone is so calm, unbothered by the fact that Armando, Ericson and me are all still a tangle of limbs.

"What the fuck?" My brows are pushed together and I'm still trying to make sense of everything when Armando's large frame stands, my body sliding off of it as gravity pulls me down.

"Welcome to the family." Pen snickers as she walks past me. "Now, I hope there's more food back in the kitchen, or Hayley here is going to whoop y'all's asses. Never fuck with a pregnant woman's food."

Hayley nods in agreement as she stares lovingly at the tray in her mother's hands. "God, these looked so good."

"Don't worry. There's plenty more in the kitchen." A laugh ripples from my throat as Armando and Ericson continue to glare at each other. "But we should definitely keep these two apart as a little preemptive damage control."

Austin groans as he returns from the tent to find both men still engaged in a staring contest. "I thought I told you two to behave."

Ericson growls unapologetically. "Any agreement went out the window the minute he put his hands on her."

"It's my job to protect her, twat-waffle. How am I supposed to do that if I can't touch her?" Armando retorts but Matthew, who'd just joined the party, isn't having it.

"Enough! This love triangle shit ends right here. Unless Poppy expressly states she doesn't want anyone touching her, then that choice is hers and hers alone to make." He walks over to his pregnant Hayley and cups her sad face in his hands. "Y'all fuck with my girl's food again, and I'm laying you both out cold. I don't give a shit if you found your mates. Nobody messes with a Crown."

Found their mates? No way in hell. Armando is hot, for sure, but he doesn't like me that way. Right?

And Ericson… Sure, he's drool worthy with that broad chest and thick arms. But he's a liar. The man kept vital information from me. There's no way my soulmate would ever do such a thing.

No. They're just testosterone filled assholes, fighting to assert their dominance over the only available female here. That's all it is, and all I'll ever let it be.

Men are trouble—all of them—and it'll be a cold day in hell before I fall for one again.

Thank you for taking a chance on Tortured Crown! If you enjoyed it, please consider leaving a review. They help me out tremendously and I'd greatly appreciate it.

MEN OF WRATH

Acts of Atonement: A Single Dad Age Gap Romance

Acts of Salvation: An Age Gap Romance

Acts of Redemption: A Second Chance Romance

Acts of Grace: A Brother's Best Friend Romance

Acts of Mercy: A Stepbrother Romance

CROWN BROTHERS

Filthy Crown: A Single Dad Age Gap Romance

Trojan Crown: A Single Dad Age Gap Romance

Sinful Crown: A Single Dad Age Gap Romance

Tortured Crown: A Single Dad Age Gap Romance

Be sure to join my newsletter so you're updated with upcoming releases freebies. There's nothing like a fresh book hitting your inbox!

join the Sinfully Seductive Newsletter here.

ACKNOWLEDGMENTS
Thank You

Wow.

It's been one hell of a ride, completing five books in two years, but I want to thank you from the bottom of my heart for going on this journey with me.

I think it's safe to say that the past two years in general have been insane for a lot of us. So much loss but also a lot of newfound love and friendship.

This book wouldn't be possible without the love,

support, and constructive criticism from my beautiful Lauren @romancensass. I love you to the moon and back, babe. Thank you for alpha reading this baby for me and for letting me know your unfiltered thoughts. You're one of kind. Seriously.

I'd also like to thank all of my wonderful bookstagram friends who kept me motivated through their love of the Crown Bros. Series. You have no idea how much it meant to me, waking up and seeing all of the lovely posts and messages you shared. Thank you Mary, Anna, Hayley, Nicole, Suny, Salina, Jennifer, Brittany, Nikki, Anne, Ali, Ari, Samantha, Kristien, and so many more. You've helped make this journey unforgettable and I appreciate each and every on of you.

A massive thank you also goes out to everyone on the ARC team. You ladies rock! Thank you for taking the time to read my babies. I know there are so many other books out there, and it means the world to me that you've taken a chance on one of mine. Thank you a million times over.

And last, but of course not least, thank you. Thank you for choosing my book baby. I hope you've enjoyed this series as much as I've enjoyed writing it. Stay tuned, babes! There's more to come.

Sending you all of my love and gratitude—always.

www.ingramcontent.com/pod-product-compliance
Lightning Source LLC
LaVergne TN
LVHW010308070526
838199LV00065B/5485